GREAT TALES OF

THE UNKNOWN

SHORT STORIES FROM MASTERS OF THE GOTHIC AND MACABRE

BY

VARIOUS AUTHORS

British Library Cataloguing-in-Publication Data
A catalogue record for this book is available from the
British Library

CONTENTS

DR IMMORTELLE

Kathleen Ludwick

GOTHIC
'"Gothic" implies a style of writing, a way of looking
at things, a sense of "innocent horror". This classic tale of
"vampirism" has all these ingredients along with a villain who
is as much an innocent victim of Dr Immortelle as any of the
children who they prey upon!'

I have to smile when I hear all this talk about rejuvenation, after the story Victor De Lyle told me, lying white and still on his cot in the hospital overlooking the ocean, the changing expression of his great dark eyes the only sign of life about him. Dr Immortelle beat them to it by about a hundred and fifty years. Strange that his theory has never occurred to any of our modern Occidental practitioners, at least not until very recently. I saw an item in the papers the other day that caused me to suspect that a European scientist had either discovered the secret for himself or perhaps gained his inspiration from the writing of the ancient alchemists, where no doubt Immortelle gained his.

I do not doubt that Methuselah lived a thousand years; I do not doubt that, barring accident, it is possible for men to live *ten thousand* years, if they so desire, or that men have done so and will do so again. Perhaps in time, longevity like that will become so universal as to be taken for granted. The process of rejuvenation will become as common as that of vaccination or the injection of the various serums and anti-toxins that are now the fad of the hour. It may even become compulsory by due process of law! It will follow naturally that the Mrs Sangsters (sic) of that day will be heard with respect and no doubt Malthus will have many statues erected to his memory.

Why shouldn't we be rejuvenated? Most of us have attained to but the vaguest conception of the meaning of life when 'the black camel kneels before the gate'. We hear a great deal about infant mortality, and it is indeed a pitiful thing: but the mortality of the mentally immature is also appalling and infinitely more tragic. But – goat's glands! The thought gives one a feeling of nausea. I wonder if the results of that same operation in olden times, as the historians say, 'shrouded by the mists of antiquity', do not form some basis for the legends of fauns and satyrs, those strange beings, half man and half goat, which figure so largely in Grecian and Latin mythology; and if, perhaps, the increasing number of such monsters did not result in the discontinuance of the operation? How shocking to become the parent of such a being! Thank heaven, there is another and better way! At least it will be better if there is wide and general knowledge concerning it for the protection of humanity. To the dissemination of such knowledge I now devote the last days of my life. For myself I do not desire longevity. Such a desire died in me when a Red Cross tent was bombed on the French frontier. Perhaps it was for this that I came, alive, out of the hell of the Argonne!

I have none of the arts of the professional writer. I know nothing of the rules of short-story writing. I am just a plain mining engineer of mediocre ability, wielding a geological pick and hammer more easily than a pen and more familiar with mortars than metaphors. I coula run a tunnel to tap a ledge in a porphyry dike easier than I could tell this strange tale. I know more about secondary enrichments than I do of the terminology and equipment of modern surgery, but if the layman can grasp my meaning, I shall be well content. Often, strangely enough, it would seem, it is the man in the street who anticipates the most astounding scientific discoveries and grasps their tremendous significance to humanity before his apparent intellectual superiors. I realise that, as Walt Whitman said of his poems, 'It will do good – it may do much evil also'. But I have faith to believe that the good will far outweigh the evil.

I started for San Francisco one May evening from my parents' home in the Santa Cruz Mountains. It was a moonlit night, and there was little traffic on the highway. The air was soft and mild and fragrant with the scent of innumerable flowers in the gardens of the homes that line the highway down the Peninsula for half-a-hundred miles. Even the humblest home in this favored region may possess the never-ending joy of flowers the year around, if nothing more than the humble petunia and the cheerful scarlet geranium. Where on the face of the globe, except on the shores of the Mediterranean, is there another section so favored by nature as that to which the inhabitants of the region bordering on San Francisco Bay all pridefully refer to as 'The Peninsula'? It is the Mecca of the whole Pacific Coast. From the north they 'go down to the Bay to get warm', from the sunny San Joaquin, and further south, they stream up to the Bay 'to cool off'!

Eastward towered the dark bulk of Mount Diablo. To my right the waters of the lower bay flashed in the moonlight. On my left rose green, gently sloping hills, with their wealth of native shrubs and trees and their plantations of eucalyptus, reminding me always of those words df Howells':

'The inscrutable sadness of the mute races of trees.'

I passed Palo Alto with its picturesque university buildings, silent witness to the good that the tragedy of one life may bring to countless multitudes; the salt heaps of Leslie shone white as snow in the moonlight as I passed. It pleased me to speculate on the appearance of the section I was traversing, when it should have been settled as long as London or Paris or Naples has been.

And so I neared the twin cities of San Mateo and Burlingame, the latter with its picturesque little railroad station. A couple of miles south of San Mateo I almost ran over a woman carrying a suitcase. I stopped and offered her a ride. Imagine my astonishment when I found it was Linnie Chaumelle. I had known her as a child in Idaho and she had grown into the loveliest woman I have ever seen. I had long ago lost all track of the Chaumelles, but a few months previously had chanced to meet Linnie at the bedside of a friend in a local hospital, where she was on duty as a special nurse, and we had renewed our acquaintance.

It was the death of Linnie's little brother, Vernon, that precipitated the exposure of that strange and sinister being, Albert Immortelle, and his assistant, Victor de Lyle, and caused them to flee from the Wood River Valley 'between two days'. Immortelle asserted that the child had cut himself and he had dressed the wound. Linnie's uncle, an eastern surgeon of some note, arrived unexpectedly for a visit about that time. An infection developed and the child died. The child's uncle openly charged that the wound had been made by a surgeon, and that Immortelle had been performing an experiment of some sort. The Chaumelles were amongst the oldest residents of that section and highly respected. Feeling ran high and threats of lynching were openly uttered. Immortelle and his assistant owned one of the first automobiles in that section. They fled in the night, and in spite of the attention excited by the appearance of autos at that time, nothing was ever heard of them again until they reappeared many years later in San Francisco.

The strangest feature of it was that my own father stoutly affirmed that he had known Dr Immortelle some forty years before and he had appeared no older at the time he left Wood River Valley. Dr Immortelle insisted that he was the son of the physician my father had known, but father was positive in his identification. And to complicate matters still further, my grandfather declared that *he* had known this same Immortelle *sixty* years before! That he recognised him because of a peculiar triangular scar above one eyebrow. Dr Immortelle asserted that this scar was a family mark – a matter of heredity: but my grandfather had served in the Civil War and knew something about wounds himself. He laughed at the idea that the scar was a hereditary mark. As he said it, it was very unlikely that a grandfather and son and grandson should have been wounded in such a manner as to result in the same identical sort of scar in the same location. Moreover, the same explanation could not apply to Victor de Lyle. Both my grandfather and my father were willing to swear to his identity, so he could not be explained away so easily. The people of the camp were frankly puzzled. Both my grandfather and my father were men of unquestioned veracity whose sanity had never been doubted; hardheaded business men of good judgement and common sense. There was some mystery here. For those still living, it will be solved if they chance to read this narrative.

No words of mine could convey a just impression of Linnie's beauty and womanly grace; she was the ideal nurse, with the physique and vitality that every nurse should possess; and besides, she possessed that dignity and nobility of character in which many nurses are sadly lacking. To meet her in such a place, at such an hour, staggering under the weight of a heavy suitcase, and in what I might almost call a disheveled condition, was inexpressibly shocking to me. She was a woman of very even temperament, but she appeared to be labouring under considerable excitement. She asked me to drive her to her apartment in the city: but after hearing a part of her story I turned the car and drove back down the Peninsula – past Los Gatos and through the canyon, to the ranch of my parents in the Santa Cruz Hills. Linnie's mother and mine had been friends in those long-past Idaho days and I knew my mother would give her the care she needed. I left her there and returned to the city.

The afternoon papers were filled with the details of the latest accident in El Diablo Canyon. Dr Immortelle, a well-known local physician, and his associate, Victor de Lyle, had been conducting a sort of orphanage or sanitarium at Crescent Beach. Starting for the city at night, they had gone over the bank, into the canyon, hundreds of feet below. The accident had apparently been caused by their swerving the car to avoid running over the body of a tramp that some other car had struck and killed. Dr Immortelle had been killed instantly and shockingly mangled, and Victor de Lyle had been fatally injured.

One of the puzzling features of the accident had been the presence of a woman's footprints near the scene of the tragedy; also the appearance of a young and beautiful woman at a little station down the Peninsula, who had appeared greatly agitated at missing the last local to the city and had started out afoot, carrying a heavy suitcase, apparently with the intention of walking to the next station two or three miles away, to catch the inter-urban ear whose terminus was at that point. The theory was advanced that the footprints had been made by a woman occupant of the car that had struck the tramp; that, getting out of the machine, she had found the tramp to be fatally injured, and because of this and possibly other compromising circumstances, she had feared to inform the authorities. The mystery was never solved to the satisfaction of the police and detectives. Only one person besides myself and parents, and the actual actors in the tragedy, ever knew who made those footprints. That was my wife. Linnie made them – Linnie, my other self, who sleeps in a little French cemetery near where the Germans bombed the Red Cross tent where she tended the wounded and dying. I promised Victor de Lyle that I would write this story as best I could, but it would not have been given to the world in her lifetime had my wife lived. I am giving it to the world now because the time for my own passing draws near and I believe the world is ready for the wide and practical application of Dr Immortelle's method of rejuvenation.

I went to see Victor de Lyle as soon as the physicians would allow me to do so. There were certain features of Linnie's story that I desired to have corroborated. Bit by bit, at the cost of the most excruciating agony, the recital spread over many days, he told me the most amazing story I have ever heard. There have been times since when I have wondered if I weren't as locoed as any Idaho steer that has been browsing on rattleweed: and then I remembered finding Linnie on the highway, and what my father and grandfather said about having known Immortelle so many years before, and thereby regain faith in my own sanity.

As a child I had always feared Dr Immortelle, the sinister-looking older man with the dark, compelling eyes, despite his efforts to win my favor: but I had always liked his young assistant, De Lyle, with the ready, sympathetic smile and gentle manners and the kind brown eyes whose expression hinted of sorrow and tragedy. I wrote down his story as he related it to me day by day. Later I read it to him and he pronounced the most vital portions correct in every detail. Since then I have consulted various authorities, talked with physicians and surgeons of international reputation, and I am assured there is no serious technical error in the tale.

I can differentiate between lancet and scapula, bistoury and cannula; I can even discuss the merits of the Aveling syringe as compared with the Collins apparatus or Spencer's instrument with the cannula that can be plunged directly into the blood-vessel. Also, I have opinions as to the merits of arterial as opposed to intravenous transfusion: but I had hard work learning to twist my tongue around such terms as phlebotomy, arteriovenous anastomosis, ambolism and thrombosis: and it was a long time before I got hep to the difference between Crile's tube and Payre's tube and Brewster's tube of German silver. This, then, is what de Lyle told me.

'I was born a slave on a plantation in North Carolina in the year 1745 No, *not* 1845. I was born a mulatto. Perhaps you think my mind is affected – but wait till I have finished! My father was a white overseer and my mother a negress from the Guinea Coast. I am not delirious – I am not insane – although I realise that it must be difficult for you to credit my statements.' Incredulously I noted his soft, waving brown hair, his hazel eyes, his skin that in health had been fairer than my own suntanned hide. 'You will believe me before my story is ended,' he said sardonically. I did.

'My old master was of French ancestry. Huguenot stock. His wife's people were Pennsylvania Dutch – and Quakers. They were in one of the great treks from Pennsylvania to North Carolina. She had not hesitated to marry outside the fait;h in which she had been reared when she met and fell in love with the elder Immortelle. Perhaps it was from her that Albert inherited that mystical tendency which influenced his life so greatly.

'The elder Immortelle was the proprietor of a large plantation. Naturally, he grew the products peculiar to that region – tobacco, cotton, corn and horses. He had been educated for a physician but he had a passion for stock raising. Being an altruist, his knowledge of medicine and the crude surgery of the times was of incalculable benefit to the inhabitants of that sparsely settled region, and he gave of his time and services as freely to the most wretched slave as to the haughty proprietor of the most widely stretching plantation. He possessed one of the finest libraries in America at that time. Among his books were some of the works of the ancient Alchemists. They possessed a strange fascination for his son. The boy would pore over them for hours when other lads of his age were engaged in riding or hunting or other local sports and pleasures usual to youths of their years.

'Second only to his interest in books was the attraction animals possessed for him, especially his father's thorough-bred herd. Even as a child he was always begging for pets. As he grew older, he would ask for them under the condition that they were to be his own exclusive property to do with as he pleased. His father was greatly pleased by the scientific spirit which Albert displayed in the breeding of the stock on the plantation. My master possessed some of the best specimens of horseflesh in that section. He fondly hoped to see his son become one of the most famous stockbreeders of his day. If he had suspected the object which no doubt inspired his son even at an early age, his emotions would have been of a different character.

'Albert turned his earliest attention to the breeding of poultry, cats, dogs, sheep and other comparatively shortlived animals, that he might observe the results of certain experiments on several generations. He was especially impressed with the disastrous results of inbreeding in relation to fecundity, and this formed the very basis of the theory he was slowly evolving and which was to be fraught with such tragic and momentous results to himself and countless others.

'Like most Southern gentlemen of that period, he was fond of gaming, wine and women: but so great was his self-control that I never knew him to overstep the bounds of sobriety. In gaming and the pursuit of women his methods were cold-bloodedly scientific; but I believe that during his whole lifetime he really loved only one woman.

'He was selfish and cruel, persistent in the pursuit of any object. He was a "throwback", a reversion to some strange type that one found it impossible to associate with either parent. His father and mother never understood him. He was an even greater puzzle to me who saw more of him than anyone else did. We were nearly the same age. His father had given me to him for his own personal attendant. It seems strange to you that I was ever a slave, doesn't it? But I assure you that it is true and I am able to verify this statement in every respect. I was his almost constant companion. For hours at a time he would pore over certain problems whose existence I did not at that time suspect. I have known few human beings, capable of such intense concentration.

'When we were young lads he said to me once:

'"Victor, when I will move my hand, why is it that my hand responds to my will? It must be for the reason that every smallest particle of that hand has a consciousness of its own!" And this was long before Dalton had advanced his atomic theory. We had never heard of molecules or atoms, to say nothing of electrons! He had no modern microscope to aid in confirming his theories. No one at that time had ever witnessed the marvelous division of cells, the orderly action of centrosomes and chromosomes with which every student of histology is today acquainted and takes as a matter of course. His error lay in his theory of the manner of reproduction of cells and yet, in spite of this, he and I are, or were, living witnesses to the success of his experimentation.

'He acquired all that the colonies had to offer at that period in the study of medicine and surgery, then pursued is studies in London and Paris and even in other capitals of Europe. I remember once in Vienna – but let that pass! I accompanied him always and for his own purposes he educated me. There never was the same prejudice on the Continent against colored people that has always existed here in America.

'We were in Paris at the outbreak of the Revolutionary War. A privateer nearly captured us on our way home. I have often wished that it had sunk us. Albert served through the war and I was with him as his personal attendant. Naturally, we were exposed to great dangers. I feel certain now that he was by nature cowardly, but his scientific bent of mind and the goal he had in view were sufficient to counterbalance his fears. He had the reputation of being one of the most fearless and efficient surgeons in the Continental Army. Strange that a man should so determinedly face death in his efforts to find a preventive of Death itself! How many revolutionary heroes lost their lives as a result of his experiments I have no means of knowing, but the total was doubtless large. I possessed a considerable knowledge of medicine and surgery, myself, for those times, which was all a part of my master's plans. He took great pains to instruct me in the anatomy of the nerves and bloodvessels.

'At the close of the war we settled in New York. We took a house in a secluded suburban section. Immortelle was then about forty years old and both of us commenced to feel the effects of years of military service with the inescapable hardships which would appear so incredibly severe to modern soldiers. My master's step was not so springy as it had been.

'Never have I seen a human being who dreaded the approach of age as did my master. It was while we were living in the New York house that he first broached the subject that must have been uppermost in his thoughts for years. I was astounded. His plans to make practical application of his theories filled me with horror, hardened to suffering as I had become during the course of the war. I am by nature conservative. Also, I had not the depth of intellect of Albert Immortelle, nor his scientific bent of mind.

'Afterwards, I could recall many hints and innuendoes that should have prepared me for his disclosure and I wondered that I had not grasped his purpose sooner. Cleverly he dangled the bait before me.

'"Remember," he would say when I wavered, "only accident can bar us from attaining any age we may desire to reach. We can remain youthful and grow increasingly attractive with the passage of the years, instead of hideously ugly with wrinkled skins and bald heads and the yellow snags of age in our mouths that ever repel youth and beauty." (Our dentists at that day were not capable of performing the miracles of artistic dental surgery that we take as a matter of course today.)

'Remember, he was my master – I his slave. Over me he had the power of life and death. Never was such a cunning tempter. He tempted me with the promise of freedom and the hope that through the gradual loss of most of my own blood, covering a long period of time, and the substitution of Caucasian blood through the process of transfusion, I might, to all intents and purposes, become a Caucasian. You cannot understand what that means, you who have not been an object of contempt and disdain through no fault of your own; you who have not been jostled brutally on the sidewalk and kicked off the curb by your actual inferiors, and felt yourself helpless to resent brutality and insult!

'Briefly, his theory was this: That the tiny particles of our bodies which we now call cells, breed and reproduce their kind in a manner somewhat similar to that of most animals; that the inbreeding through countless generations, ih the body of a human being which they themselves compose, causes a loss in fecundity just as it does in horses and cattle; causes the cells to degenerate, to "run out", as we say of animals and plants; *and that this loss in fecundity is the true cause of old age*. He believed that, as stock men range far afield for new strains to strengthen the breeds of their flocks and herds, so new vigor might be acquired by introducing young and vigorous cells into the blood of the aged. *Necessarily, the cells to be so introduced must be from the vascular system of youth*; and even then, I think, he glimpsed the truth which science has but lately demonstrated, that the character of the blood of an individual becomes fixed at the age of three or four years and thereafter remains constant.

'There is no doubt that the ancient Alchemists practiced this method of rejuvenation. Immortelle's error lay in his theory as to the manner of reproduction of the cells, which, instead of breeding with older cells in the veins of the recipient, simply mutiplied through division in their new locations crowding out the weaker cells, and went about their tasks of rebuilding the body with new materials and removing the waste products.

'Tranfusion is old – how old no man can say. It was probably practiced long before recorded history. A friend of mine who has accompanied several archeological expeditions to the Far East asserts that the Alchemists gained their knowledge from the secret records of a fraternity old before Babylon and Nineveh became but rubbish heaps covered by the shifting desert sands! It is a fact that transfusion was employed in the case of Pope Innocent VII, and there is a tradition to the effect that three young boys perished in the attempt. Perhaps the old legends of vampirism had their origin in such a source.

'Transfusion is a common operation today, but when Albert Immortelle first broached the subject to me, an open announcement of our object would have been regarded with the greatest horror and only too well-founded fear of results would have rendered it impossible for us to secure subjects. Anesthetics had not yet been discovered and aseptic surgery was a hundred years in the future. We had to devise ways and means of securing subjects.

'It was my young master's plan to found an orphanage, whose most promising inmates he would later use for his transfusion experiments, which heretofore had included animals only. I was to be his first subject after the children; and when I had mastered the details of the process, he himself would submit to the operation. Of course, the danger as well as the suffering was incalculably greater than in these days of anesthetics and aseptic surgery. My master was skilled in – the art of hypnotism, or mesmerism, as it was then called, but it often failed. Probably he was the first surgeon to use that strange force for anesthetisation. It is a well-known fact that children are less susceptible to it than adults; and our subjects were all children, mostly of tender years – in fact all that *survived* were of such tender age! Tales of children of such age would in any event be treated as due to vivid imaginations. Even to this day I sometimes waken from nightmares with the agonised screams of those little victims ringing in my ears.

'Today there is practically no danger from infection and the danger from clotting is being eliminated through the division of humanity into groups classified according to the constituency of their blood. We had no aspirating syringe to determine the amount of blood taken from the donors and how many little victims lost their lives in this manner, as sacrifices to our rejuvenation, I have no means of knowing. It was, of course, unwise to keep records of such cases. All I know is that there were many fatalities. How we escaped with our own lives is a mystery to me. I am unable to fathom the inscrutable purpose of Providence in allowing us to cumber this earth for so long a time.

'When my conscience revolted, always before my eyes

Immortelle dangled the bait of my own altered personality; for I had emerged, a radiant Caucasian, from my somber and repellent negroid chrysalis. As far as I am personally concerned, from a physical standpoint, I am, or rather was, a living witness to the success of his experiment. Even the most widely experienced ethnologist would hardly suspect me of having one drop of negro blood in my veins. No one who had known me as a kinky-haired mulatto youth, were he in existence still, would ever recognise that colored boy in the cultured, refined Caucasian with the waving brown hair, hazel eyes and complexion as fair as your own, with the rosy hue of health in his cheeks. From a selfish and brutal young savage with a violent temper, I had been transformed into an amiable and tractable individual, vastly useful to my master, but more conscientious than was conducive to my peace of mind or his. This was due, I am sure, to Immortelle's deliberate selection of children of most amiable disposition for donors in transfusion operations in which I was the recipient. For himself he always selected fearless and intrepid subjects of indomitable wills. Such wills are often characteristic of amiable children. Stubbornness and strength of will differ from each other as widely as the poles.

'For the sake of greater safety, to be more reasonably certain that the blood of the donor would assimilate with my own, Immortelle always bled me freely before a transfusion.

Immortelle deserves credit at least for his scientific accomplishments. Intellectually he was a giant amongst the men of his time. When he commenced his experiments he had no safe and sure scientific ground beneath his feet. He was treading the insecure and shifting sands of conjecture.

'Always he emphasised the ultimate benefit to humanity of our experiments; but for many a long and lonely year I realised that his own chief object was to live as long as possible, in order to gratify his sensual appetites, however Epicurean they might have been termed, to the limit of danger to his hold on life.

'Every man with a drop of blood in his veins has a passionate desire for offspring. Several times I contemplated marriage, but Albert always discouraged me.

'He argued that if we married and had families, we must either witness the passing from life of our wives and offspring, or witness their endurance of the sufferings and dangers of transfusion. We knew nothing of aseptic surgery, but I believe my master grasped the principles of it before we commenced our experiments, for he always used bottled water and the scorched linen dressings that so many regarded merely as a superstition of old midwives.

'There was always the danger of thrombosis due to the admixture of certain bloods which refused to assimilate. Immortelle argued with good grounds for his conviction, that it would be impossible to rejuvenate our wives and offspring even to the second generation, without knowledge of our methods becoming known. Someone amongst such a large group would inevitably give the secret away. Also when a hue and cry were raised, as was bound to be the case sooner or later, it would be difficult, if not impossible, to escape from popular wrath with a large number of relatives and dependents. It had been difficult enough on several occasions for our two selves. So reluctantly I relinquished my dream of conjugal felicity – the tender joys of one's own fireside, for the Dead Sea fruit of immortality in the flesh. I realised my error many long years ago: for I have come to know that immortality for the individual isolated from his kind could not atone for the loss of the happiness conferred by a perfect and harmonious union and the sweet delights afforded by the companionship of one's own offspring.

'Of course it was impossible to conduct an orphanage without attendants, and more especially female attendants. Ours were chiefly young women who had been saved by Immortelle and myself. They were obviously curious when assisting at transfusion operations, but their curiosity was never satisfied. The trained nurse had not as yet been evolved when we commenced our experiments in rejuvenation.

'Naturally all our philanthropic efforts to save the reputations of the erring were not successful. Usually they covered their tracks in coming to us and always bore an assumed name. When they departed, only Immortelle and I knew how, or when, or what their destination was. We had many aliases, he and I, but used our own names most frequently. It was embarrassing to meet people one had perhaps known forty years before. In such cases, he often passed for a son of himself, as in Idaho, where, however, he failed to deceive your father.

'In spite of all, suspicion would fasten on us. Rumors would spread connecting us with various mysterious disappearances. We found it expedient to leave our New York address on one occasion, more hastily than was convenient. So it was with our Philadelphia orphanage and others we established in this country. It was the same with those we established in London, and in Paris and other Continental cities. In some locations we spent as long a period as ten years. In others no sooner were we established than some catastrophe would occur, which would spoil all our plans and send us scurrying into hiding. This was the case when we were compelled to depart so hastily from that quiet and comparatively isolated valley in Idaho, where you and I first met – you a child and I to all appearances a young and inexperienced physician, but in reality an old and saddened man with experience of agonies unparalleled by any other person save my master, Immortelle! On him they had apparently no effect.

'In that little Idaho mining camp everything seemed favorable to our plans. It was a small camp and yet not small enough to allow each resident to become extremely familiar with the private affairs of all the rest. There was a considerable floating population, as in all mining camps, which was an advantage from our point of view.

'The absolute privacy essential to the successful prosecution of our plans was possible in the house we chose amongst the magnificent old cottonwoods of the river bottom and from which that beautiful but brawling stream derives its name. Earth does not hold a more picturesque spot than that narrow valley walled in by the precipitous mountains of the Sawtooth range. Often I close my eyes to see quite vividly again those miles on miles of cottonwoods. I recall the contrast of their orange hues in autumn with the dark green of the hardy firs that venture bravely down into the valley so far from most of their kind, and I see the thousands of ears of flame-colored chokecherry brush. And in the early summer, who that has ever seen them can forget those acres upon acres of blue forget-me-nots? In that valley they seem to disregard their naturally retiring habits that lead them to choose their abodes in the shelter of trees and shrubs. Away from all shelter, they boldly advance into the valley and flaunt their vivid hues under the blue skies of Idaho!

'Our house, as you remember, was an old, flimsy,

unpainted weatherbeaten structure, but easily and cheaply remodeled for our purpose, ostensibly that of residence and laboratory. Immortelle was supposed to be deeply interested in the study of chemistry. Naturally, in such a climate, where the cold is so intense for a long period of each year, deep cellars are indispensable. We constructed a large one, also an underground laboratory with double skylight and heavy shutters which would prevent freezing of our chemicals and also serve to muffle any undesirable sounds and outcries.

'The river bottom consisted chiefly of gravel in which a small grave might easily and rapidly be dug at dead of night, if necessary. Also, the cottonwoods and thickets of wild roses, chokecherries and other shrubs hung with the creepers of the wild clematis, screened us in summer from inquisitive eyes and permitted easy access to a certain disreputable quarter of the camp. It was always possible in case of urgent necessity to secure assistance from this quarter, for there are always some nurses amongst those unfortunates. Dr Immortelle never passed up anything. In return for his professional services he was usually able to obtain assistance that was almost as invaluable as his own. We were acquainted with the details of many a tragedy hidden from the knowledge of the general public. As you may know, it was the discovery by two little girls of the grave of a newborn infant, richly clad, in the gravel of the river bottom, together with the death of little

Vernon Chaumelle, that precipitated our flight.

'There never was any necessity, from a financial standpoint, for Dr Immortelle or myself to practice our professions. The proceeds from the sale of his father's plantation, to which he was the only heir, had been invested in Manhattan real estate nearly a hundred years before, as well as my own salary after the Emancipation Proclamation. The doctor's profession was only a blind, only a cloak for our real and sinister purposes.

'A considerable space of time is naturally required to establish a physician in a new location. Immortelle usually employed some length of time injudiciously cultivating the acquaintance of the local "four hundred", many of whom, sooner or later, he was absolutely certain, would require his professional services. It fell to my lot to make the acquaintance of the oldest inhabitants and, through them, to familiarise myself with the history of the best of families, chiefly in regard to heredity, persistently recurring physical characteristics and freedom from blood taint of a certain character.

'The densely wooded river bottom furnished an ideal playground for the children of the camp. There were long stretches of clean white sand and gravel to play in; Indian paint brush to suck honey from; thickets of wild roses, willow clumps for shade with violets hidden in the lush grass of their shady recesses, coral flowers and fragrant red mallow. An ideal spot also for two human vampires to find a childish victim!

'Not being on the main line of the railroad, that section was rarely visited by tramps at that time, although at long intervals they used the willows for a camping ground. Down there in the willows we assiduously cultivated the friendship of the little ones through stories we told them, and the judicious gifts of sweets. We finally decided upon a donor for the next transfusion operation in which Immortelle was to be the recipient. Carefully we spun the threads of our web.

'The Chaumelles were amongst the oldest and most respected residents of that section. There was no blood taint in the family. They had been clean-living and high-thinking people for generations. One of the children, Vernon, met all but one of the doctor's requirements. He possessed no trace of cruelty, and he was a hundred per cent perfect from a physical standpoint. He was courageous, strong-willed, but not stubborn, and of more than average mentality. He was then scarcely five years old and Linnie, his little sister and constant companion, was a little over three. They often came to play in the willows wiih older children. One day they ran away by themselves from their home at the opposite edge of town. They were playing in the grove near our house when Vernon fell and hurt his arm. It was a mere scratch and really needed no attention. By dint of a little candy and considerable persuasion, we succeeded in getting them inside the house, little golden-haired Linnie, with the wide, wondering blue eyes, and dark-eyed, sturdy little Vernon.

'Linnie was left in our living-room, while Immortelle *extracted the splinter* from her little brother's arm. A box of chocolates and some wondrously illustrated story books, purchased purposely for such occasions, occupied her attention for awhile; but tiring of them, she found her way unexpectedly, through a door carelessly left unlocked, to our subterranean operating room. I have never been able to forget the expression of her great blue eyes when she saw me in my white smock and cap, surrounded by the implements of my murderous occupation, and her little brother strapped securely to one table under the influence of the imperfect anesthetic, his pale face becoming ever paler as the life stream flowed from his little artery through the glass tube into the vein of the sinister-looking man reclining on the other table beside the child's couch. We were not yet using an aspirating syringe, which would allow us to measure the quantity of blood lost by the donor, and were alarmed by the pallor and weakness of the little boy. Even the two hardened creatures who assisted at the operation seemed frightened and conscience-stricken.

'I carried Vernon home, his little pale face resting on my

shoulder. I had concocted some plausible tale to account for the prolonged absence of the children. The whole camp had been searching for them. I told a story of a fall and a wound caused by a piece of tin from an old can left by some hoboes at their camp, and a serious loss of blood. I promised to call next day and dress the wound in case it seemed inexpedient to take Vernon to the office. Dr Immortelle was indisposed, having injured himself with a lancet in dressing Vernon's wound. What a hypocrite I felt; how vile I knew myself to be, when they thanked me so profusely for my *kindness*!

'You know what happens sometimes to the best laid plans of mice and men. Perhaps you recall the incident that led to our undoing; how Vernon's uncle, an eastern surgeon of some note, arrived unexpectedly on a visit and himself dressed the wound; how his suspicions were aroused. You remember how an infection developed and the child died, and how almost simultaneously the grave of a newborn infant was discovered in suspiciously close proximity to our "laboratory". Perhaps you can recall the investigation that followed. You may remember that a sort of catacombs was later discovered connecting with our operating-room, several bricked-up niches and their gruesome contents; but before that we were well on our way to safety. We owned one of the first automobiles in that part of the country.

'Your father declared that he had known Immortelle *himself* forty years before in the East, and not the latter's *father*, as Immortelle had always insisted; and to cap the climax, your grandfather solemnly averred that *he* had known this same Immortelle *sixty years before*, and that at the time he appeared in Wood River Valley, he appeared no older than at the time your grandfather had known him in his youth! One factor in his recognition and his positive identification consisted of a peculiar triangular scar over the left eyebrow. Had it been a birthmark it might have appeared for several generations; but it was improbable that three generations would meet with an accident resulting in the same identically shaped scar in the very same location. Some who had known your father and grandfather well for many years were frankly puzzled. They knew them for men whose reputation for truth and veracity had never been questioned. Others were greatly amused and operily accused them of being the victims of hallucinations. They made sarcastic references to the Wandering Jew, to St Germaine, to Lord Lytton's well-known hero, Zanoni, and that lesser-known but no less remarkable character of fiction, Melmuth the Wanderer.

'After some years we returned to San Francisco. Both of us were younger in appearance than when we fled from Idaho. Also, there were several little graves in the Argentine, whose occupants, if they could have spoken, might have thrown considerable light on the source of our youthful appearance and whose piteous tales would have wrung the hearts of humanity and brought down swift and terrible retribution on the vampires who had waxed young and strong on their suffering and the sacrifice of their young lives.

'It was not long until Immortelle was practicing successfully again, with a numerous and fashionable clientele. He soon acquired a reputation for philanthropy by contributing princely sums to various orphanages and other charitable institutions for children, and was always ready and willing to attend the little unfortunates they harbored, giving his services freely and without charge. Also, he did much charity work amongst the children of the poor, although not nearly so much as he was given credit for doing. I myself did a large portion of the work he was credited with. He was known to be deeply interested in the study of heredity and was a specialist in blood transfusion, which becomes increasingly safer, because of the continuous progress in aseptic surgery and the classification of humanity into groups according to the constituents of their blood.

'When at last his reputation seemed firmly established, he purchased an old house in the midst of a large, wooded acreage close to the ocean shore and within sound of the breakers, many miles south of the city. It had formerly belonged to an eccentric and wealthy recluse, who had chosen this secluded situation for his retirement. The advent of the automobile had changed conditions somewhat and a highway ran a comparatively short distance from the place. The house was an old, rambling structure. It stands on a rocky promontory overlooking the ocean, surrounded on two sides by a tall, thick cypress hedge. Little did the passing motorists dream of the stairs that led down through solid rock to a tunnel connecting with the ocean, and in which a stout boat was always moored.

'It was here that we established an orphanage and sanitarium for a small number of children, after thoroughly remodeling the old place. For these children Immortelle had conceived a deep and eternal interest and affection, but he sometimes remarked, with the most wistful expression and in an extremely melancholy tone, that no sooner had he become deeply attached to one of his young protegés than Fate would operate in some strange way to deprive him of their companionship – a fact which I thoroughly understood and was well able to confirm. He might also have added that Fate had seen fit to deprive him of the services of several nurses who had assisted at transfusion operations which had terminated unfortunately.

'Of course all our philanthropic efforts to avert disgrace did not terminate as we could desire. There were a number of mysterious disappearances of young women from that region which have never been explained to the satisfaction of – shall we use the stereotyped formula of "the police" or the "general public"? But in the public mind our own institution was never connected with them in any way until that accident in Deep Canyon.

'During the influenza epidemic, beautiful Linnie Chaumelle entered into our lives again, Linnie whom we had known as a child in Idaho and whose little brother Vernon had virtually met death at our hands. All the nurses in San Francisco were either in attendance on victims of the epidemic or ill themselves when it made its appearance at our orphanage. Linnie had chosen the career of a trained nurse. There is no finer or nobler under heaven. Her parents had both died when she was quite young and the family had become widely separated. Very likely she had forgotten the names of Immortelle and myself. Albert engaged her without a personal interview, contrary to his usual habit, on the recommendation of a brother physician. It was something we had never done before, but our need was urgent. When they met, it was obvious to me, who knew him so well, that with Dr Immortelle, the selfish, cynical, absolutely conscienceless man of the world, it was a case of love at first sight!

'It was not to be wondered at. Linnie Chaumelle is the most beautiful woman I have ever seen during more than a century and a half of evil living. She could well have served some great artist as the model for an angel, with her roseleaf skin, her masses of chestnut hair with its glints of gold framing her lovely face; and those large, limpid blue eyes, through which one may glimpse her radiant soul.

'As time passed, it became increasingly evident that, for the first time in his evil existence, Albert had fallen victim to that little god who is no respecter of persons. Day by day I watched his love for Linnie grow. He vainly endeavored to exert his undoubtedly great hypnotic powers over her, but no evil power could affect that pure spirit that occupied a plane so vastly superior to his own. I had determined, in any event, that her mind should be kept free from the octopus-like tentacles of his hypnotic powers at any cost to myself.

'As I have said, all our philanthropic efforts did not terminate as successfully as we could have desired. It was while Linnie was at the sanitarium that one of the disastrous terminations occurred. Linnie is not naturally suspicious, but she is a young woman of more than average intelligence. As a nurse, she possesses from observation a wide knowledge of evil in countless manifestations; but her own soul has remained uncontaminated. She had not been there long before various circumstances combined to arouse her suspicions.

'I have mentioned a subterranean passage. It was convenient in case of emergency; and yet we found that stout ropes and even chains attached to pallid bodies of unfortunates and anchored by heavy weights have been snapped asunder by the violence of the breakers on that rocky coast. It was an incident of that nature that led to Immortelle's decision to dispose otherwise of the remains of a young and beautiful unfortunate and that likewise led to our undoing. Fate is a tricky hag! I should say, more correctly, what I now know to be the truth, that the time was at hand for reaping what we had sown.

'We had spent most of the previous night in digging a grave in the mellow soil of a small, isolated country place down the Peninsula. The ground belonged to me and I objected to this use of it, but my objections were silenced as usual by Immortelle. We removed the mute witness of our evil deeds from the sanitarium under cover of darkness, as we supposed, without the knowledge of any of the inmates except the one nurse attendant on that case. We had no reason to fear that she would make any damaging disclosures.

'Immortelle placed the poor body in the rear seat and sat beside it, supporting it in an upright position, while I drove the car. As I have said, he was by nature cowardly, and not all the transfusions from the veins of courageous donors had ever overcome this tendency. A large touring car followed us somewhat closely. Immortelle suspected that they had some suspicion of our sinister design, or that they might contemplate a hold-up. I think he was entirely wrong, but at any rate he became greatly agitated and was thrown into a perfect paroxysm of terror. His great black eyes rolled like the eyes of a maniac, his pallid face forming a startling contrast to his raven hair. His forehead was covered with great drops of perspiration and he was shaking as if with an ague. In any event, they could hardly have overtaken us. Our car was specially constructed for speed – as a physician's car should be, of course! Only we knew what speed it was capable of attaining. But he was terror-stricken, incapable of reasoning.

'"Faster! Faster," he screamed, as I drove the car at dangerous speed around sharp curves on the brink of a five-hundred-foot precipice. We managed to elude our pursuers, if such they were, by turning off into a little-used road and waiting until they had passed; then we turned back into the main road. Never have I seen a human being in such a panic. In spite of my remonstrances he made me stop as close to the brink as possible, where the canyon wall fell away below us for hundreds of feet, and compelled me to assist in pushing the poor girl's body over the edge into the abyss below. Then we re-entered the car and drove on to the city.

'In the ordinary course of events, the corpse would have remained undiscovered for years, perhaps until identification had become difficult, if not impossible; but in avoiding Scylla, we had become engulfed in Charybdis. Some Boy

Scouts climbed down into the canyon next day to recover a lost hat and made the gruesome discovery of the remains!

'The papers were full of pictures of the poor victim who was not identified for a considerable space of time. They were full of supposed details of the crime. We felt comparatively safe, as only one of our nurses had been in attendance on the victim and we had every reason to feel sure of her discretion and loyalty. We had taken special precautions in regard to the arrival at the sanitarium of the girl now dead, so we felt confident that only the three of us had seen her there; but it happened that, of all persons in the world, Linnie had by accident, through the opening of the wrong door on a certain occasion obtained a passing glimpse of her and recognised her picture! She went to Immortelle at once. Her wonderful eyes rested steadily on his as she said:

'"I will ask you to take me to the city immediately, Dr Immortelle."

'He remonstrated, but it was useless, so he agreed that we should take her in to the city that evening. Then he laid the hideous plan in which I apparently acquiesced.

'"She knows too much, now!" he said, his face distorted with rage and fear. "She must be silenced!" I shuddered. I had heard those words from him so many times in the course of close to a hundred and fifty years. I am certain he had come to feel the same towards me because of my increasing repugnance toward the course we were pursuing, which must have been obvious to him. My awakening conscience must have become a source of alarm to this man, himself without even the vestige of such an inconvenient faculty. I believe that he had planned my removal, as soon as it could be conveniently accomplished and he could secure the assistance of a confederate to take my place.

'We owned a cabin in a secluded nook, not far from the road, yet far enough to prevent any sounds of terror or agony from being heard by passing motorists. It had proven convenient for our purposes on more than one occasion. Its windows were heavily shuttered and it was surrounded by dense shrubs and trees, so that its existence would ordinarily have remained unsuspected by passers-by. Immortelle proposed that we should start for the city with Linnie. We were to develop engine trouble when opposite the cabin. Knowing that Linnie would not care to remain alone with him on the highway, such was the repugnance with which he evidently inspired her, I was to go to the cabin for the tools we should find necessary, and she was to accompany me. The rest would be easy, he judged from certain past experiences of a similar nature. After she had been drugged and rendered insensible and was at his mercy – after she had been kept at the pleasure of his will as long as suited his purpose, he judged she would become sufficiently tractable. Her own few remaining relatives were far away and she would probably not be missed for an indefinite period.

'I had an entirely different plan. I revered Linnie as I have never revered any other woman. I instinctively sensed the incorruptible purity of her soul, her unlimited sympathy of that maternal character which persists, though even in the very slightest degree, in the most debased and corrupted specimen of femininity. I would gladly have given my life to save her from him. I had no hope that she would ever care for me – no desire to bind her pure life to mine, with its innumerable crimes. I had ceased to crave for continued existence. The many crimes in which I had been Immortelle's accomplice, although for years unwillingly, lay heavy on my conscience. From myself the world had nothing more to fear; but the conscience of Immortelle was unawakened. He was a menace to humanity. I decided that the greatest service I could render humanity would be to put an end to his career, even at the sacrifice of my own life.

'We left the orphanage that evening after dinner. I was driving. Linnie occupied the seat beside me, refusing to sit in the rear seat with Immortelle, where, unknown to herself, only a short time before he had supported the body of a victim. Not far from the cabin that was to be her destination, and not far distant from the place where we had thrown the body of the young nurse over the canyon wall, I ran over a pedestrian. He was a tramp, clad in khaki-colored clothing – you know its low range of visibility – but we might have avoided striking him had it not been for the excessive speed at which we were traveling.

"'Drive on! Drive on, you fool!" screamed Immortelle as I stopped the car. All of us got out. The man was fatally injured but he still breathed.

"'Dead!" said Albert nonchalantly. He took the victim by the feet and dragged him out of the road.

"'Get in!" he ordered, as Linnie stood there, white with horror.

"'Surely you will not leave him there!" she gasped. "The man is not dead."

"'He is only a tramp! What difference can his life or death make?" snarled Immortelle.

"'He is a human being! If you leave him here you will leave me with him!" she said defiantly. The spotlight shone on Immortelle's face. It was black with rage and murderous. *And then Linnie remembered!*

"'I know you now, you fiend!" she said, and took a step nearer and shook her finger accusingly at him.

"'*You are the man who killed my little brother!*'

'Immortelle snarled like a trapped animal. There was the flash of steel in his hand; but before he could spring on Linnie with the knife, I had struck him on the head with a revolver. Then I trussed him up with a tow-rope and a dog-chain we had in the car. The tramp had breathed his last. I dragged both of them into the bushes. I put Linnie into the car.

'"I will return for them," I said in answer to her unspoken question. We started for the nearest little railroad station, thinking she could catch the midnight local to the city. On the way I gave her the barest outline of this story. She is a nurse and acquainted with the marvelous results of transfusion, with all the latest aids and discoveries of the scientific medical world. Perhaps she thought me a mere madman, but I fully believe she accepted my story and had faith in my repentance. I made her promise to say nothing *until she should hear from me again.* I wanted to keep her name out of the papers. You know what they are. We had engine trouble in truth and it was late when we reached the outskirts of the little station where she was to take the train. Immortelle and myself and our car were well known there and I judged it best, in spite of the lateness of the hour, for her to proceed alone.

'"You will probably never see me again," I said at parting. "Think kindly of me sometimes, if you can."

'"Do not go back!" she begged. "I am afraid for you! He will kill you!"

'Perhaps she sensed that bit of good in me which persists

in the most hardened. I had saved her. Perhaps she grasped my plan, telepathically, and shrank from its accomplishment, for her forebears have been law-abiding people for many generations. I took her hand and kissed it. The little innocent, with an impulse which sprang from her recognition of my genuine repentance, her gratitude, and her own strong maternal instinct of protection, put up her pure lips for me to kiss, she with her lily-white soul and I with my soul as black as my face once was! I was not fit to touch the hem of her garment with my lips, but I kissed her once. Nothing can erase the memory of that kiss. That second of supreme bliss was enough to recompense me for all I must face here and in the hereafter. I know you do not begrudge it to me, you who are destined to be her matte. Remember that, though I have practically become Aryan in body, my soul is still that of an Ethiopian – and colored people have strange moments of clairvoyance, whose reason is known only to the occultist.

'I drove away and left her. I have seen death in countless forms; I have been an accomplice, times without number, in what practically amounted to murder under the guise of scientific experimentation; I have witnessed scenes of horror whose remembrance fills me with an agony of remorse; and tears had been strangers to my eyes for what seemed like ages; but when I drove away and left her there, I could hardly see to drive for the blessed tears that filled my eyes.

You know what happened – that she was too late for the local and started to walk to San Mateo, carrying her heavy suitcase. And how you came along and picked her up, thank God!

'I returned to the spot where I had left Immortelle and the body of the tramp. It makes cold chills run up and down my spine even now when I remember the look in Immortelle's eyes when I turned my flashlight on him where he lay bound and gagged. His eyes seemed to emit veritable flashes of venomous light. I almost quailed before him, bound and helpless as he was; but the thought of Linnie put courage into me. And I realised that my failure to carry out my plan meant death for me. My one fear was that someone would come along before my work was done, but there was little traffic over that road at night.

'"Now I am going to drive both of us over the cliff," I said. "If it were not for dragging *her* name through the mire, I would surrender myself and you to the authorities. But Justice is sometimes slow and uncertain. My plan seems the surest. I do not hold myself less guilty than yourself, although you were the greatest criminal in the beginning. However, I awoke, long ago, to the enormity of our crimes and would have endeavored to atone, in some measure, had you allowed me to do so. I have never been able to detect the slightest evidence of repentance in you. I wish it were possible for you to meet the fate you so richly deserve, in full possession of your faculties, but I dare not risk it. I shall be compelled to give you a few shots in the arm to insure your good behavior, for I shall have to unbind you to make the execution appear to be an accident." Almost it seemed that he would break even the stout chain in his frantic struggles to escape the awful fate that threatened. I drove the needle in deliberately, and often enough to render him incapable of resistance.

'I placed the tramp in the middle of the road. Then I lifted Immortelle into the machine, backed down the road some distance, came on at the rate of forty miles an hour or more, swerved the car as if in an effort to avoid running over the body of the tramp, and the next instant we were falling through space – down – down—

'You know how they picked up Immortelle, crushed and battered out of all semblance to his former self; how a tree broke my fall and they found me with my head and face unmarred, but with my back broken by the boulder I struck. Obviously, the papers all agreed, and I later corroborated them, that it was an accident due to the driver's swerving the car sharply in an effort to avoid running over the tramp. The most puzzling feature was the presence of a woman's footprints at the scene of the tragedy, a mystery which has never been solved! A possible solution was that the tramp had been struck by a hit-and-run woman motorist, who, finding that her car had killed the pedestrian, after getting out and examining him, had driven away and feared to report the accident.

'Immortelle's vast fortune will revert to the State, as he left no heirs. My own fortune I have left to be used for scientific and medical research, more especially with regard to blood transfusion and its free and scientific application for the benefit of suffering humanity.

'Sometimes as I lie here, I wonder if evil, or what we call by that name, *is* ever employed in the scheme of things for good ends. Can it be needed, like the substance we place at the roots of flowers to cause them to bloom more luxuriantly and more radiantly? Well, I shall soon know!' he said with that prescience of approaching death with which I was so soon to become familiar on the battlefields of France. He passed away that night.

Before I left him he made me promise to give his story to the world, believing that in proper hands, under scientific supervision, transfusion might prove of tremendous value to humanity; that it might be employed, not only to rejuvenate, but to repair and remedy both physical and mental defects. I have done my best. As I have said in the beginning, I am only a mining engineer, more familiar with the symbols of mineralogy and chemistry than with figures of speech.

Linnie and I both went across to France soon after our marriage. I remember the night we left San Francisco, There was no moon. The waters of the Bay were like a pool of black ink in which the vari-colored lights of the ships were reflected. To the south, a huge electric sign showed blood-colored through the smoke of some giant smokestack where men toiled in the sweat of their brows 'to make the world safe for Democracy!'

A wisp of smoke from a passing steamer was wrapped around the Ferry tower, almost concealing it, and above it the light on its summit shone like a symbol of Hope; but the Germans bombed the Red Cross tent where Linnie ministered to the sorely wounded! Although I escaped alive from the hell of the Argonne, I lie here almost as helpless as Victor de Lyle when I saw him last, longing for the time when my soul shall be reunited with its mate.

THE PASSING OF VAN MITTEN

Claude Farrère

WEIRD

'The story of a man who passed through the death agony,
to learn – what?'
Weird Tales, 1938.

When the priest had administered extreme unction, he
went away. Van Mitten had only a short time to live, there
was not the slightest doubt about that. There was no one in
the room with him now but the old nurse. The poor woman,
who had been under a strain for days, had fallen sound asleep
in her chair. Strangely enough, although the end was so near
at hand, Van Mitten was completely and lucidly conscious.
He was not suffering in the slightest. His life was ebbing
away, that was all. He was an old man, and his vital forces
were dying out. He had lived life to the full, for as long as
his physique had been able to carry him. The machine was

worn out, and in a few hours or minutes the wheels would cease turning.

The dying man's eyes wandered about the room. He had spent many a night within these four walls. Twenty thousand perhaps, or thirty thousand. He tried to calculate, but what was left of his mind was too feeble. His yellowish hands lay side by side on the counterpane. He tried to cross them on his breast, but that was a task completely beyond his strength. For all practical purposes, he was dead already. There was nothing to do but lie there and wait. Wait and think.

Death – The thing was certainly much less terrible than he had supposed it would be. He had been afraid of it in the past, very much afraid of it. Now, now that he was coming face to face with it, the bugaboo did not seem so frightful, after all. A very small thing, to be sure. The mountain was bringing forth a mouse, as had happened so often in the course of his life. He did not feel the slightest fear of it, only curiosity. So this much-discussed hour was about to strike for him, very shortly. And after it struck – what then? There was certainly something more! Annihilation? Or another life?

He had not devoted a great deal of time to speculation during all the years of his long life. Van Mitten had never been what is called a religious man, but neither had he been what is called an atheist. He had been one of those men who take things as they come – who don't understand about the eternal matters, and who make no particular effort to do so. But the moment had come when the eternal matters had to be faced. Evasion was possible no longer. What would happen to him next. Where would he go, what would he be, after he had passed the experience called death?

'I haven't the slightest idea,' he said to himself, as he lay perfectly motionless, unable even to open his lips. 'I don't know, and nobody knows, and no living person has ever known. But I shall know very soon – I shall know what no living person has ever known!' But at no moment in all the period of waiting, he was sure of it, had there been the slightest sensation of fear. Van Mitten wondered at this, passively and coolly. Then he wondered at another thing – at a strange, regularly recurring sound which had suddenly penetrated his consciousness, and which seemed to be somewhere very near him.

He thought: 'What extraordinary rhythm is this?'

But in a moment he understood. The sound was in his own body. It was in his own throat, in his own breathing. It was a phenomenon which he had read about, which he had even heard once or twice before, himself. It was the death-rattle.

'Well now!' he thought calmly. 'So the death-agony has begun?'

The more he thought of it, the more surprised he was. He had supposed that the death-agony was invariably something very painful. But search through his consciousness as he might, he could not discover that he was suffering in the slightest.

In the meantime, the old nurse had awakened. Several other persons had come in – relatives and friends. The little bedroom was crowded with them. The dying man was still able to see, but he saw everything and everybody with perfect unruffled indifference. He was not clear about who all these visitors were. A sort of fog seemed to be coming over his vision. But he had no particular desire to recognise any of them. In this last moment: of life, he was interested only in himself. One curious question held all his feeble attention, to the exclusion of all other thoughts and feelings: What was coming to him next? Nothing? Something? What?

His lips made a vague effort to frame the assurance, for himself alone:

'I shall know very soon – I shall know certainly – I shall know everything – *everything* . . .'

But the only visible and audible effect of his effort was an increase in the violence of the death-rattle. Someone who stood beside him murmured:

'Ah, how he is suffering!'

Van Mitten heard the words and would have been glad

to make a sign that the speaker was mistaken; but he had not the power to move a muscle. His eyes grew dimmer and dimmer. And he noticed that his hearing was dulling.

Some time passed. Minutes. Many minutes. The dying man no longer saw anything at all, no longer heard anything. Then he had the sensation that he had made an entirely involuntary motion; it seemed to him that his hands had stirred as if to draw the bed-clothing up toward his face. His thoughts were full of confusion, but he remembered one thing distinctly:

'Ah, yes! my hands lay on the counterpane – in front of me . . .'

He felt a resurgence of curiosity, and he began again to study his sensations and emotions. No, there was no doubt about it; he was not afraid. But his interest in his situation, in spite of the tenuous and as it were muted condition of his thinking faculties, seemed to grow keener and keener, as he felt that he was approaching nearer and nearer – it could only be a matter of seconds now – to the supreme moment. It was all very strange, almost unbelievable. For a moment, he felt a flash of incredulity that it could be he, and not someone else, that lay here on this bed, on the point of passing out of life. Well, his life had had a beginning, and it had to have an ending – that was logical, wasn't it? Logical? *Was* it logical, after all? Perhaps it wasn't so inevitable! Was it true that his life had had a beginning? What did he know about it?

He was conscious that someone had held a mirror in front of his mouth. Someone, the physician no doubt, said solemnly:

'He's gone!'

And Van Mitten knew that the person was right. He knew that an eternally valid change had taken place, that he was now what men call dead. He said to himself – and he realised perfectly well that he no longer had any voice, any lips, to say it with – he repeated to himself: 'Now I shall know! Now I shall know everything!' But he was filled with an immense astonishment to discover that he did *not* know. He did not know anything at all! Death had torn away no veil. The mystery of things remained intact, impenetrable – just as it had been before!

He was bewildered, baffled, helpless with perplexity.

'What is this?' he said to himself. 'What is this? I am dead. There is no doubt about that. I am completely, thoroughly, irrevocably dead. I am not annihilated – I am still *I*, just the same – I still have being, I am immortal – but what a strange sort of being it is! I can't see, I can't hear, I can't feel, I can't remember – What is this, what is this? What am I? What was I? Where did I come from?'

He was plunged into an ocean of ignorance. He tried hard to think, he had the power of effort and he made use of that power, he seemed to himself like a bird fluttering against the bars of his cage. Then it seemed to him that he saw the reason for his helplessness.

'My memory – my memory was left behind – so of course – well, even if *it* is gone, I am still a person, I am still myself.'

Now he realised that it was impossible, that his speculations could arrive nowhere. He surrendered, completely. He understood that it could not be otherwise. His memory belonged to his past, to his completely separate past, his past which was in no sense he any longer. He would never be able to remember his past life, he would never be able to know that he had been something before, something different – a thing, even a person – in the past that was past for ever and ever.

All of a sudden he discovered that he was very, very tired. He relaxed and let himself sink, physically as well as mentally. And under him, he had a confused feeling that springs were yielding, the springs of a soft bed. Was he dead no longer? Dead. What did the word mean? Nothing, nothing at all. He reached out his hands – by what miracle did he have hands, and could he thrust them out? – he felt clumsily of smooth, braided willow work, to the right, to the left, braided osier walls – he tried to speak, but could not – he had no words – he had no thoughts, even – he could remember nothing – he knew nothing – it was all strange to him, all new, prodigiously new and difficult.

Yet he had a voice. He could make a sound. His voice sounded like:

'Wah! . . . wah! . . . wah!'

Someone came to him. A voice called, hopeful, troubled:

'Is he all right? I thought I heard him crying.'

And another voice replied:

'He's hungry, that's what's the matter with him! He's fit as a fiddle, bless his heart! I'll bring him to you so he can get his dinner!'

And the person who had been Van Mitten, who had grown old and died and been born again, sucked down his fill of mother's milk and went to sleep again.

THE RIVER OF DEATH

Fred M. White

TERROR
'A deadly poison was drawing ever nearer to the great
metropolis of London, carried in the waters of the gently
flowing River Thames . . .'
Pearson's Magazine, 1904.

The sky was as brass, a stifling heat radiated from stone and wood and iron – a close, reeking heat that drove one back from the very mention of food. The five million-odd people that go to make up London, even in the cream of the holiday season, panted and gasped and prayed for the rain that never came. For the first three weeks in August the furnace fires of the sun poured down till every building became a vapour bath with no suspcion of a breeze to temper the fierceness of it. Even the cheap press had given up sunstroke statistics.

The drought had lasted since April. Tales came up from the

provinces of stagnant rivers and quick, fell spurts of zymotic diseases. For some time the London water companies had restricted supplies, but there was no suggestion of alarm. The heat was almost unbearable but, people said, the wave must break soon and the metropolis would breathe again.

Professor Owen Darbyshire crawled homewards towards Harley Street with his hat in his hand, his grey frock coat showing a wide expanse of white shirt below. There was a buzz of electric fans in the hall, yet the atmosphere was hot and heavy. There was one solitary light in the dining-room – a room all sombre oak and dull red walls as befitted a man of science – and a visiting card glistened on the table. Darbyshire read it with annoyance: 'James P. Chase, *Morning Telephone.*'

'I'll have to see him,' he groaned, 'but is it possible these confounded pressmen have got hold of the story already?' Doubtless Chase was merely plunging around after sensations – the constant pestering of newspapermen was no new, thing to Darbyshire with his reputation for fighting disease in bulk, the orie man always sent for when there was an epidemic to be grappled with. Still, the pushing little American might have stumbled on the truth. When he came back, he had better be granted an audience, however brief. Meanwhile Darbyshire took down his telephone and churned the handle.

'Are you there? Yes, give me 30795, Kensington . . . That you, Longdale? Step round here at once, will you? Yes, I know it's hot, and I wouldn't ask you to come if it wasn't a matter of the last importance.'

He hung up his receiver, lighted a cigarette, and proceeded to con over some notes. He was roused presently by the hall bell and Dr Longdale entered. 'I suppose it's come at last?' he asked.

'Of course it has,' Darbyshire replied, 'and in a worse form than you think. Just listen to this:' and he took from his pocket a newspaper clipping.

STRANGE AFFAIR AT ALDENBURGH

A day or two ago the barque *Santa Anna* came ashore at Spur, near Aldenburgh, and quickly became a total wreck. The crew of eight presumably took to their boats, for nothing has been seen of them since. How the *Santa Anna* came to be wrecked on a clear, calm night remains a mystery. From the thousands of oranges which have been picked up at Aldenburgh lately, the coastguards presume the barque to be Portuguese.

'Naturally you want to know what this has to do with us. Well, the *Santa Anna* was deliberately wrecked, and the crew for reasons of their own sank their boat. It isn't far from Aldenburgh to London: in a short time the Portuguese were in the metropolis. Some of them set off for Cardiff, to get a ship there. On the way three are taken ill, two of them die. The local practitioner sends for the medical officer of health. The latter gets frightened and sends for me. I have just got back – with *this*.'

Darbyshire produced a phial of cloudy fluid, some of which he proceeded to lay on the glass of a powerful microscope. Longdale fairly staggered back from the eyepiece. 'Bubonic! The water reeks with the bacillus! You don't mean . . .'

'I do. This sample comes from the Thames. Those seamen, who ran their ship aground and deserted her, have been suffering from bubonic fever – and by a series of circumstances they have infected the river which gives most of London its water supply. That deadly poison is hourly drawing nearer to the metropolis into which presently it will be ladled by the million gallons. People will wash in it, drink it, Mayfair along with Whitechapel!'

'The supply must be cut off!'

'And deprive four-fifths of London of water when it is grilling like a furnace? No flushing of sewers, no watering of roads, not even a drop to drink. In two days London would be a reeking, seething hell – try and picture it!'

'There's only one alternative – that process of sterilisation of yours.'

Darbyshire smiled, and moved towards his office. The notes were there, but they seemed to have been disturbed.

On the floor lay a torn sheet with shorthand cypher: thereon Darbyshire flew to the bell and rang it violently.

'Verity,' he cried when the butler appeared, 'has that Mr Chase been here again?'

'Well, he have, sir, just after Mr Longdale. So I asked him to wait, which he did, then he come out again after a bit, saying he would call again, looking very excited, sir.'

'It's clear enough,' Darbyshire turned to Longdale. 'That confounded journalist has heard all we said – and tomorrow the whole thing will be blazing in the *Telephone*. Those fellows would wreck the empire for a "scoop". But we can perhaps convince the editor that that article must not appear.' He called the butler again. 'Get me a hansom, fast as you can.'

A minute later there was a rattle of wheels outside and Darbyshire plunged hatless into the night. 'Offices of the *Telephone*. A sovereign if I'm there in twenty minutes.'

The cab plunged on headlong. The driver was going to earn that sovereign or know the reason why. He drove furiously into Trafalgar Square, a motor car crossed him recklessly, and a moment later Darbyshire was shot out onto his head. He lay there with no interest in mundane things. A crowd gathered, a doctor in evening dress appeared.

'Concussion of the brain . . . By jove, it's Darbyshire! Here, police, hurry up with the ambulance: he must be removed to Charing Cross Hospital at once.'

The controlling genius of the *Telephone* sat limp and bereft of coat and vest. His greeting of Chase was not over-polite. But when he saw the sheet of notes that the journalist carried, the tired look faded from his eyes. Here was the tonic his soul craved for.

'It wants pluck . . . A scare like that might ruin the Empire.'

'Take it or leave it. If you haven't got the grit, Sutton of the *Flashlight* will jump at it.'

Grady made his decision. 'Sit down right away and make two columns of it. I'll get some statistics out for you.'

Cold facts made the story seem worse, rather than better. The upper waters of the Thames were poisoned – yet nearly all London derived its water supply from those waters. Only two London water companies did not derive their water from the Thames – the New River Company and the Kent Company. Only those fortunate enough to be served by these mains would be exempt from peril – and even they would soon be in danger from their neighbours.

The further Grady read, the more he felt that if he could get this dread information into the hands of the people before it was too late, he would be playing the part of a benefactor. Desperate as the situation looked, the *Telephone* might yet save it. Professor Darbyshire had no right to hold up such a secret when he should have been taking measures to avert the threatened danger.

An hour later the presses were roaring: presently huge parcels of damp sheets were vomited into the street. London awoke, and on a hundred thousand breakfast tables the eye was arrested by scare heads:

THE POISONED THAMES

Millions of plague germs flowing down into London. Bacillus of bubonic plague in the river. New River and Kent Companies alone can supply pure water. Stupendous discovery by Professor Darbyshire. Death in your breakfast cup today. Shun it as you would poison. If you are not connected with either of the above companies, or if you have no private supply – CUT OFF OUR WATER AT THE MAIN AT ONCE!'

At eight in the morning London's pulse was calm and regular. An hour later it was writhing like some great reptile in the throes of mortal pain.

The one man who could have done most to help was lying unconscious at Charing Cross Hospital. Meanwhile Dr Longdale was the man of the hour – but he could not allay the panic that had gripped London. Under a blazing sunshine after days of heat and dust the packed East End was suddenly deprived of every drop of water. For an hour or two no great hardship was felt, but after that every moment added to the agony. Before long the railway termini were packed with people eager to be away from the metropolis.

By midday business was at a standstill. There was not a water cart to be seen from Kensington to the Mansion House. Every cart and tank had been despatched into the New River and Kent Water area to convey a supply as speedily as possible to the congested districts East and South-east of the Thames. By lunchtime the City presented a strange spectacle. Well-dressed business men could be seen proceeding in cabs with buckets and water cans with the object of taking a supply forthwith. Cabmen were commanding their own prices.

Mineral waters went up 200 per cent in price: by midday the supply had ceased – men of means with an eye to the future had bought up the whole stock. The streets were crowded with people anxiously awaiting developments. They were rewarded a little after two o'clock when a boy came yelling down the Strand with a flapping of papers on his shoulder: 'The plague broken out! Two cases of bubonic fever at Limehouse! Speshull!'

Perhaps if the readers had known these two cases were renegades from the *Santa Anna*, the panic might have been allayed. But nobody knew. Though no fever could have broken out so soon, it was assumed that the two poor fellows had drunk of the polluted flood and paid the penalty. It might be the turn of any of them next. There were those who shrugged their shoulders stolidly, others that crept into bars and restaurants and asked furtively for brandy.

By this time everything that could be done was being done. The artesian wells of East and South London were being tapped. Private houses which possessed pumps were besieged. Main line trains made way for trains of tanks bringing water to the city. But the problem of distribution remained – how could the little water available be distributed fairly among six million people over an area of some thirty square miles?

Night came, but brought no end to the stream of people coming and going between Trafalgar Square and such other open supplies as were available. Morning brought the promise of another sweltering day. Smartly dressed men were to be seen with grimy chins and features frankly dirty. The dust in the unwatered streets became intolerable. Tempers were strained. Small riots broke out here and there, some people were robbed of their precious fluid as they carried it home. Democratic agitators took advantage of the situation, a mob stormed the Houses of Parliament singing the Marseillaise in strident tones. Looters ravaged the markets, went off with baskets of apples and oranges. Mysteriously, as the sign that called up the Indian Mutiny, the signal went round to raid the public houses and hotels. Men stood in the Strand outside famous restaurants with bottles of strange liquids in their hands, the necks of which they knocked off without ceremony to reach the precious fluid within.

What might have happened when these last scant resources gave out will fortunately never be known. For suddenly, beneath the hubbub of the streets, the clamour and shrieks of the rioters, a strange unbelievable sound was heard. The shouting died away – and the people of London heard it now with no mistaking: the sound of water! The water supply had been restored!

The turncocks in the Strand were busy flushing the gutters with standpipes, a row of fire engines were proceeding to wash the streets down from the mains. The whole thing was so sudden and unexpected that it seemed like a dream.

And what was even less expected – what people only learnt when they read their papers that evening – was that the city's water supply was safe to drink all these days. For what Dr Darbyshire had no time to tell his colleague, in his hurry to get to the *Telephone* offices, was that as soon as he realised the pollution of the water at Ashchurch, he had applied his sterilising process on the spot. A few miles further down the river, the water gave the result of perfect purity.

But for the accident in Trafalgar Square, there would have been no untoward consequences: but Dr Longdale, having seen the bacillus-infested water, and not knowing of the sterilisation, had no alternative but to cut off the water supply forthwith.

London that night was in a frenzy of elation. Men shook one another by the hand, hats were cast into the air and forgotten: people stood under the beating drip of the fire-engines' sluicing until they were soaked to the skin: well-dressed men laved themselves in the clear running gutters. London was saved from disaster, and Dr Darbyshire was the hero of the hour.

'All the same, it was a near thing, Longdale. Some day perhaps this country will realise what a debt it owes to its men of science – and perhaps learn to foster them a little more. For nothing but science could, these past days, have prevented a calamity that would have multiplied ten-fold the horrors of the Great Plague, and destroyed not thousands, but tens of thousands.'

MORNING ON THE WISSAHICCON

Edgar Allan Poe

MACABRE
'*Wrapped in half-slumberous fancies, the man watched a
vision of the most extraordinary nature . . .*'
The Opal, 1844.

It was not until Fanny Kemble, in her droll book about
the United States, pointed out to the Philadelphians the rare
loveliness of a stream which lay at their own doors, that this
loveliness was more than suspected by a few adventurous
pedestrians of the vicinity. But, *the Journal* having opened all
eyes, the Wissahiccon, to a certain extent, rolled at once into
notoriety. I say 'to a certain extent,' for, in fact the true beauty
of the stream lies far above the *route* of the Philadelphian
picturesque-hunters, who rarely proceed farther than a
mile or two above the mouth of the riverlet – for the very
excellent reason that here the carriage-road stops. I would
advise the adventurer who would behold its finest points to

take the Ridge Road, running westwardly from the city, and, having reached the second lane beyond the sixth milestone, to follow this lane to its termination. He will thus strike the Wissahiccon, at one of its best reaches, and, in a skiff, or by clambering along its banks, he can go up or down the stream, as best suits his fancy, and in either direction will meet his reward.

I have already said, or should have said, that the brook is narrow. Its banks are generally, indeed, almost universally, precipitous, and consist of high hills, clothed with noble shrubbery near the water, and crowned at a great elevation with some of the most magnificent forest trees of America . . . that define the moss-covered bank, against which the pellucid water lolls its gentle flow, as the blue waves of the Mediterranean upon the steps of her palaces of marble. Occasionally in front of the cliffs, extends a small definite *plateau* of richly herbaged land, affording the most picturesque position for a cottage and garden which the richest imagination could conceive. The windings of the stream are many and abrupt, as is usually the case where banks are precipitous, and thus the impression conveyed to the voyager's eye, as he proceeds, is that of an endless succession of infinitely varied small lakes, or more properly speaking tarns . . .

Not long ago I visited the stream by the route described,

and spent the better part of a sultry day in floating in a skiff upon its bosom. The heat gradually overcame me, and resigning myself to the influence of the scenes and of the weather, and of the gently moving current, I sank into a half slumber, during which my imagination revelled in visions of the Wissahiccon of ancient days – of the 'good old days' when the Demon of the Engine was not, when picnics were undreamed of, where 'water privileges' were neither bought nor sold, and when the red man trod alone, with the elk, upon the ridges that now towered above. And, while gradually these conceits took possession of my mind, the lazy brook had borne me, inch by inch, around one promontory and within full view of another that bounded the prospect at the distance of fifty yards. It was a steep rocky cliff, abutting far into the stream, and presenting much more of the Salvator character than any portion of the shore hitherto passed. What I saw upon this cliff, although surely an object of very extraordinary nature, the place and season considered, at first neither startled nor amazed me – so thoroughly and appropriately did it chime in with the half-slumberous fancies that enwrapped me. I saw, or dreamed that I saw, standing upon the extreme verge of the precipice, with neck outstretched, with ears erect, and the whole attitude indicative of profound and melancholy inquisitiveness, one of the oldest and boldest of those identical elk which had been coupled with the red men of my vision.

I say that, for a few moments, this apparition neither startled nor amazed me. During this interval my whole soul was bound up in intense sympathy alone. I fancied the elk repining, not less than wondering, at the manifest alterations for the worse, wrought upon the brook and its vicinage, even within the last few years, by the stern hand of the utilitarian. But a slight movement of the animal's head at once dispelled the dreaminess which wrested me, and aroused me to a full sense of the novelty of the adventure. I arose upon one knee within the skiff, and while I hesitated whether to stop my career, or let myself float nearer to the object of my wonder, I heard the words 'Hist! Hist!' ejaculated quickly but cautiously, from the shrubbery overhead. In an instant afterward a negro emerged from the thicket, putting aside the bushes with care, and treading stealthily. He bore in one hand a quantity of salt, and, holding it towards the elk, gently yet steadily approached. The noble animal, although a little fluttered, made no attempt to escape. The negro advanced; offered the salt; and spoke a few words of encouragement or conciliation. Presently, the elk bowed and stamped, and then lay quietly down and was secured with a halter.

Thus ended my romance of the elk. It was a *pet* of great age and very domestic hotels, and belonged to an English family occupying a villa in the vicinity.

THE SPIDER'S EYE

Fitz James O'Brien

UNCANNY

'I found, presently, I was penetrating into what they
really *were*. A few minutes showed me what had been their
occupations for the day, and what were their plans for the
next. I saw, *at once*, all their regrets and ambitions.'
Putnam's Magazine, 1856.

There are whispering galleries, where, if the ear is placed
in a certain position, it takes in the sound of the lowest
whisper from the opposite side of the room. But, to produce
this effect, the architecture of the apartment must be of a
peculiar nature, and, especially, the rules and laws of sound
must be observed.

I have often thought that, were one wise enough, there
might be found, in every room, a centre to which all sound
must converge. Nay, that perhaps such a focus had already
been discovered by some one who has wished to appear

74

wiser than his neighbors, who has made use of some hitherto unknown scientific fact, and has on any one occasion, or on many occasions, thus made himself the centre of information.

These ideas occurred to my mind when I arrived the other night early at the theatre, and was for a time, literally, the only occupant of the house. I fell to marvelling at the skill of the architect who has been so successful in the acoustic arrangements of this theatre. Not a sound, so it is said, is lost from the stage upon any part of the house. The lowest sob of a dying heroine, in her very last agony, is heard as plainly by the occupant of the back seat of the amphitheatre, as are the thundering denunciations of the tragic actor in the wildest of gladiatorial scenes.

I wondered , if this were one of those rules that worked both ways; if the stage performer, in a moment of silent by-play, could hear the sentimental whisper of the belle in the box opposite, as well as the noisy applause of the claqueur in the front seat. If so, the audience might become, to him, the peopled stage, filled with the varied and incongruous characters.

Then if art can produce such effects upon what we call an ethereal substance – if the waves of air can be compelled to carry their message only in the directions in which it is taught to go – what influence would such power have on more spiritual media? In other worlds, where it is not necessary for thoughts to express themselves in words, but where some more subtle power than that of air conveys ideas from one being to another, it is possible that an inquiring being might place himself at some central point where he might gather in all the information that is afloat in such a spiritual existence.

Full of these thoughts, and my head, perhaps, a little bewildered by them, I passed unobserved into the orchestra, and ensconced myself in a little niche under the music-desk of the leader. I was surprised to find myself in a little cavity, from which there were loop-holes of observation into every part of the house, while there was a front view of the stage when the curtain should be raised. Seduced by the comfort of this little nook, and my speculations not being of the liveliest nature, it is not to be wondered at that I fell into a gentle sleep.

I was aroused presently by the baton of the leader, struck with some force upon the desk over my head. I was aware, at the same time, of a whispering all around my ears, and an incessant noise, like that of aspen leaves in a summer breeze, which, in spite of its softness and delicacy, overpowered the sound of the loud orchestra. When I was able to recover myself, I began to find that I had indeed placed myself in the centre of the house; not in the centre of sound, but, if I may so express myself, of sensation. I was not listening to the conversations, but suddenly found myself the confidant of the thoughts of all the occupants of this well-filled house. I was lost in the multiplicity of ideas that were poured in upon me, and endeavored to concentrate myself upon one series of thoughts. I looked through my loop-holes, and presently selected one group towards which I might direct the opera-glass of my mental observation.

There sat the five Misses Seymour. We had always distinguished them as the tall one, the light-haired one, the one who painted in oils, the one who had been south, and the little one whom nobody knew anything about. This individuality had been our only guide after having engaged Miss Seymour for a dance, and this was sufficient. The one who painted in oils always refused to dance; the one who had been south spoke with an accent, and said '*chick'n*' and '*fush*', if the conversation turned upon the bill of fare; and the others were distinguished by their personal appearance.

Now I felt anxious to discover more certainly which was which. I found, presently, that instead of contenting myself with the superficial layer of thought over my mind, created by the circumstances in which they were placed, I was penetrating into what they really were. A few minutes showed me what had been their occupations for the day, and what were their plans for the next. I saw, at once, all their regrets and ambitions.

It had been the day of Mrs Jay's famous matinée. I had not been at the reception, but Frank Leslie had told me all about it, and that all the Seymours were there; and about Miss Seymour's fainting. I knew Frank was in love with one of the Miss Seymours, but I never had found out which, and I was not sure that Frank himself knew.

How suddenly did these five characters, whom before I had found it difficult to distinguish, stand out now with differing features. I saw Aurelia – that was the tall one – enter the drawing-room very stately in her beauty. No wonder that everyone had turned round to look at her; to admire her first, and then criticise her, because she seemed so cold and statue-like. But tonight she was going over the whole scene in her thoughts. I heard the throbbing of her heart as in memory she was bringing back the morning's events. She had refused to dance, because she was sure she should not have the strength to go through a polka. She had preferred to sink into a seat by the conservatory, and upheld y the excitement of the music to await the meeting.

Oh! in this everyday world, where its repeated succession of events is gone through with in composure, how easy it is to control the wildest passions. A conventional smile and a stiff bow are the draperies that veil the intensest unspoken emotions. It was under this disguise that Miss Seymour was to greet Gerald Lawson. He went to Canton three years ago, and before he went she had promised to marry him. She promised one gay evening after 'the German'. She had been carried away by the moment. Ever since, all through the three years, she had been regretting it. It was a secret engagement. The untold feeling that had prompted it had never been aired, and died very soon for want of earth and light. To cold indifference for the man to whom she had promised herself, had succeeded an absolute aversion. What was worse, she loved another person. Aurelia Seymour loved Frank! This very morning the news had reached her that the *Kumshan* was in from Canton. The passengers had arrived last night; she was to meet Gerald at Mrs Jay's this morning.

Frank Leslie seated himself by her. She was in the midst of a calm, cool conversation with him, when she saw a little commotion in the other corner of the room. Everyone was greeting Mr Lawson on his arriving home. He is making his way through the crowd; he comes to her, he bows; Aurelia smiles.

But this Was not all. He asked her if she would come into the conservatory. She had accompanied him there. Half hid by the branches of a camellia-tree all covered with white blossoms, she had said coldly, 'Gerald, I cannot marry you.' But Gerald had not received the word so coolly. He had burst out into passion. First he had exclaimed in wonder, next he could not believe her.

'Would she treat him so ungenerously? Was she a heartless flirt, a mere coquette?'

He told of his love that had been growing warmer all these three years; of his ambition that was to be crowned by her approval; of his lately gained wealth, valued only for her sake. Passionate words they were, and full of intense feeling; but hidden by the camellia, restrained and kept under from fear of observers. They were frequently interrupted, too.

'Thank you – ninety-nine days; very quick passage. Yes, I go back next week; no, I stay at home,' were, with other sentences, thrown in, as answers to the different questions of those who did not know what they were interrupting.

But, at last, Aurelia broke away. Broke away! No; she accepted Middleton's proposal to jgo into the coffee-room, and left Gerald beneath the camellia.

As I watched her from my loop-holes I could tell that Aurelia was going over all this scene in her mind. While her eyes were fixed upon the stage, she recalled every word and gesture of Gerald's. Yet, his reproaches, his just complaints, hardly weighed upon her now. She was looking on the vacant seat beside her, and wondering when Frank would come to take it.

But 'Lilly', the light-haired one, her thoughts were rushing back to the wild, gay polkas of the morning. Now by Aurelia's side, now away again; she had danced continually till the last moment, and when they came to tell her the carriage was ready, and she must come away, she had fainted.

It was as she was going upstairs into the drawing-room, just before she and her sisters made their grand entrée, that Lilly had heard that 'Cousin Joe' had not come home in the vessel with Gerald Lawson. He had gone to Europe by the overland route, and wild, mad fellow that he was, had determined to join the Russian troops in the Crimea.

'And be shot there for his pains,' Frank Leslie added carelessly.

Cousin Joe hadn't come home! He didn't care to come home! He was going to be shot!

She could think of nothing else. She could not keep still; she could not talk placidly like the rest; she must dance, and dance wildly and passionately.

But a moment of reaction came. When the last strain of music had died away, all power of self-control had died away, too. No wonder that she had fainted! More wonder that she could recover herself; could resist her mother's entreaties, after all that dancing, to spare herself and stay from the opera.

Here she was, outwardly lively and radiant, chatting with Lieutenant Preston, inwardly chafed at all this constraint, and wondering how it was Cousin Joe could stay so long away.

By her side sat Annette. It was the report that she had been sent south last winter to break up a desperate flirtation she was carrying on. However it was, I had always fancied Annette more than either of the other sisters. She had apparently less of our northern reserve, whether for good or evil, than the rest. She said just what she was thinking; danced when she liked; was insolent when she pleased.

Tonight she seemed to me fretful. She was angry with Lilly for talking with Lieutenant Preston; and, indeed, I must not, in honor, reveal all I read in Annette's mind. If I found there her opinion of me; if, on the whole, it lowered my opinion of myself, I must take refuge, in the old proverb, 'Eavesdroppers never hear any good of themselves'.

But there was Angelina; she was the one who 'painted in oils', and she attracted me more than any of the others. There was about her an atmosphere of pleasure, within her an expression of delight, that accounted for the really sunny gleam upon her face. Something had made all the day happy for her. In the morning she had passed nearly all the time in Mrs Jay's front drawing-room. The fine masterpieces of art, brought from Europe, make this apartment a true picture-gallery. But Angelina's pleasure, artist though she was, was not taken from the figures upon the walls. She walked up and down the room; she lingered awhile in one of the deep fauteuils; she paused before the paintings with Frank Leslie by her side. As she turned, at the theatre, now and then to the vacant seat behind her, next Aurelia's, her anticipation was not embittered by anxiety; she knew he would come in time. Oh, Frank! you did not tell me *all* that took place at Mrs Jay's!

But, from all these observations, my thoughts were turned back to the stage by the influence of the little Sophie Seymour. She – about whom we knew nothing – she was the only one of the party entirely absorbed in the opera. Her eyes fixed upon the stage; her heart wrapt up in the intense story that was being enacted; her musical soul throbbing with the glorious chords that swelled out; her whole being reflected the opera.

So I turned me to the stage. My eyes fell first upon the substitute that the illness of Mademoiselle – required for the night. Just now she was standing on one side, and as she drew her white glove closer, *her* thoughts were going back to the scenes of the day.

Oh! what a little room she lived in! She was sitting in it when the message came from the manager to summon her to sing tonight! Her brother Franz was copying some music by her side; and now she is smiling at the recollection of the conversation that had followed upon her accepting the manager's unexpected proposal.

She had hastened to get out her last concert dress. It was

new once – but oh! would it answer now for the opera?

Those very white kid gloves! They had cost her her dinner.

'Must I have new ones, Franz?' she had asked. 'If there were only time to have an old pair cleaned – if, indeed, I have any left worth cleaning!'

'Never mind,' answered Franz, 'it is worth twenty dinners to have you hear the opera. I have longed so every night to have you there, and to have you on the stage! my highest wishes are granted. Oh! Marie, when you make a great point, I shall have to take my flute from my mouth and cry bravo!'

'Oh, don't speak of the singing. It takes away my breath to think of myself upon the stage! How I waste my time over dress and gloves! I must practice; I must be ready for the rehearsal.'

'My poor Marie! Today, of all days, to go without dinner.'

'Don't think of it! When the manager "pays up", oh, then, Franz! we'll have dinners. Only part of the money must go to a new concert dress. When my last was new, I overheard, as I left the stage, a young girl saying, to her sister, I suppose, "What an elegant dress!" I wanted to stop and ask her if she thought it were worth going without meat for a month.'

And as Marie recalled these words tonight to her mind, I

saw her look up and smile as she glanced over the house, and contrasted the showy dress she wore with the poor home she had left behind.

What a poor home it was, indeed! What a contrast did the gay dress she arranged for the evening make with her room's poor adorning. The dress she thrust quickly away, and had devoted herself to the study of the music for evening. With her brother's assistance, she had prepared herself for the rehearsal, and had gone there with him.

The rehearsal was more alarming to her than the thought of the evening performance. There were the conductor's criticising eyes glaring at her; the unsympathising glances of some of her, stage companions – though many of them had come to her with words of kindly encouragement; there was the silent, untenanted expanse of the theatre before her – none of the excitement of stage scenery, or the brilliancy of light and tinsel; and she must force herself to think of her part, as a technical study of music, all the time she felt she was undergoing a severe criticism from Mademoiselle—'s friends, who were comparing the newcomer's voice with that of their own ally.

But her thoughts were not sad. There was in her a gaiety and strength of spirit that bore her up. The brilliant scene gave her an excitement that helped her to bear the thought of her everyday trials. It had been hard to work all day, preparing for the evening – hard for the mind and body – and she had lately lived on poor fare, and wanted the exercise upon which her physical constitution should support itself. At once these troubles were forgotten. Now was to come the duet with the prima donna.

No timidity restrained her now. She felt, at the moment, that her own voice was of worth only as it harmonised with the leading one. She forgot herself when she thought of that wonderful voice, when once she found her own mingled in its wonderful tones. Now she was supported by it through the whole piece; her own was subdued by it, and at last she felt herself inspired by it; it was no longer herself singing; she was carried away by the power of another, and lifted above herself.

All applauded the magnificent music and harmony; the *bravo* of Franz was for Marie alone.

At this time my interest was absorbed in my observation of the prima donna. I had perceived at first how indifferently she, had entered upon the spirit of the music. Her companion had filled her mind with the meaning of its composer, and was striving to infuse into herself the interpretation that the prima donna would give to its glorious strains.

But the soul of the prima donna was away. It was in a heavily curtained room, where there were luxury and elegance. Here she had all day been watching by the bedside of her sick child. She had collected round it everything that money could bring to soothe its sufferings. There were flowers in the greatest profusion; these were trophies of her last night's success; and on the table by the bedside she had heaped up her brilliant, gorgeous jewels, for their varied and glowing colors had served to amuse the child for a few minutes. She had sung to him music, that crowds would have collected to hear, had they been allowed. Only to soothe him, all the golden tones of her voice had poured out – now dropping in thrilling, ^ad melody, now in glad, happy, childish strains.

Nothing through the day could put to rest that one appeal, which now was echoing in her ears: 'Will nothing cool my throat! – my head burns! – only a few drops of water!' Over all the tones of the orchestra these words sounded and thrilled so in her ears, that only mechanically could the prima donna repeat the tones that were thrilling all the hearts to which they came.

At last the power of her own voice conquered herself, too. In the closing cadences – in those chords, triumphant and faith-bringing – for the moment her own sorrows melted away, and the thought of herself was lost in the inspiration of the grand, majestic intonations to which she was giving utterance. She was no longer a suffering woman; but her soul and her voice were sounding beneath the touch of a great master-spirit, and giving out a glowing music, compelled by its master-power.

What an enthusiasm! What an excitement! As with the opera-singer on the stage, so with all the audience; all separate joy and grief, all individual passions were swallowed up, and carried away by this all-absorbing inspiration, and lost in its mighty whirl.

For me, now, there was but one character to follow. How grandly the stage-heroine went through her part! As if to crush all other emotion, she flung herself into the character she was portraying, and went through it wildly and passionately.

She overshadowed her little rival – for Marie was her rival, according to the plot of the opera – now threatening, now protecting her, as she was led on by the spirit of the play. Marie shrunk before her, or was inspired by her; and her delicate, entreating figure helped the pathos of her voice. Marie, by this time, had utterly lost herself in her admiration of the great genius who was so impressing her. She gave out her own voice as an offering to this great power. For its sake she would have found it impossible to make any mistake in her own singing, or do anything with her own voice, but just place it at the service of her companion, as a foil to her grand and glorious one.

When in the play the heroine gave up – as she does in the play – her own life for the sake of her rival, the act became more magnanimous and wondrous as being performed for this little delicate Marie, who shrank from so great a sacrifice.

The prima donna gained all the applause. Indeed, it was right – for it was her power that had called out all that was great in her delicate rival. It was she who had inspired her, and made her forget herself and everything but the notes she must give out, true and pure.

They were both called before the stage after the grand closing scene; or rather the prima donna drew forward the retiring Marie. Shouts and peals of enthusiasm greeted the queen of song. But her moment of exaltation had passed away. Over and over again she was repeating to herself, 'Will they never let me go home? Perhaps he is dying now – he wants me – I am too late!'

She was at the summit of her greatness; but oh! it was painful to see her there – to see how she would have hushed all those wild, enthusiastic shouts for the sake of one fresh childish tone; how she would have exchanged all those bursts of passion to make sure of a healthy throb in that child's pulse. All this enthusiasm was not new to her. It was part of her existence. It was a restraint upon her now, but she could not have done without it. It was the excitement which would serve to sustain her through another night of watching.

Marie, too, was given her meed of praise, as she followed her across the stage. She did not think of taking to herself one shout of the enthusiasm, any more than she would have thought of appropriating one flower from the bouquets which were showered before her. There was, indeed, one share of the plaudits which belonged to her entirely. This came from Franz – for I recognized him by his unruly stamping, and unrestrained applause. His thoughts were only for Marie; he was filled with pride at the manner in which she bore herself – at her simple carriage, and modest demeanor. His praise was all for Marie. The famous opera-singer, whom he had heard night after night, was forgotten, in his pride for his little sister.

I sank back into my niche. Varied figures floated before me, and bewildered me.

I have often looked at spiders with deep interest. It is said that the^r eyes are made up of many faces. What a bewildering world, then, is presented to their view! It is no wonder that, as I have seen them, they have appeared so irresolute in their motions, darting here and there. A world of so many faces stand around the spider, towards which shall he turn his attention? He lives, as it were, in the middle of a kaleidoscope, where many figures are repeated, and form one great figure, and each separate section is like its neighbor. Which of these varied yet too similar pictures shall he choose?

At least this is my idea of the sensations of a spider; but I am not enough of a naturalist to say that it is correct. How is it? When a fly enters that web, which is divided into a symmetry similar to that of the faces of a spider's eye, does mine host, the spider, see twenty-five thousand similar flies approaching, his organ of vision standing as the centre? What a cosmorama there is before him! What a luxurious repast might not his imagination offer him, if his memory did not recall the plain truth that dull reality has so often disclosed to him! We cannot wonder that the spider should lead, apparently, so solitary a life, since his eyes have the power of producing a whole ball-room from the form of one lady visitor. Not one, but twenty-five thousand Robert Bruces inspired the Scottish spider to that homely instance of perseverance, which served for an example for a king. As he hangs his drapery from one cornice to another, the prismatic scenes that come before him serve to lengthen that life which might seem to be cut off before its time. It is not one, but twenty-five thousand brooms which advance to destroy his airy home; to invade his household gods, and bring to the ground that row of bluebottles which his magnifying power of vision has transformed from one to twenty-five thousand! nay, more, perhaps!

Out in the air, as he swings his delicate cordage from one tree to another, he does not need to wear a gorgeous plumage; this old dusty coat and uncomely figure, that make a child shrink and cry out, these may well be forgotten by him who looks into life through prismatic glasses. Every drop of rain wears for him its Iris drapery; the dew on the flowers becomes a jewelled circlet; and the dazzling pictures brought by the sunbeams outshine and transform for him his own dusky garment.

I thought of my friend, the spider, as into my web of thought came such numerous images. They were not alike in form – and so were more distracting. More than I can mention or number had visited me there; had excited my interest for a moment, and been crowded out by another new image. Yes, it was like looking into a kaleidoscope where there were infinite repetitions. In all were the same master-colors and forms. All were swayed by passions that made an under-current beneath a great outward calm. All were wearing an outward form that strove each to resemble the other; not to appear strange or odd. So they flitted before me, coming into shape, and departing from it as they came within and left my reach.

I only roused myself to see the various characters, that had presented themselves on the stage of my mind, return again into their everyday costumes. They passed out of the focus of my observation into their several forms in which they walk through common life. Putting on their opera-cloaks, their paletots, they put on, for me, that mark that hides the inner life, and the veil that conceals all hidden passions.

It is said that there is, no longer, romance in real life. But the truth is that we live the romance that former ages told and sang. The magic carpet of the Arabian tales, the mirror that brought to view most distant objects, have come out of poetry, and present themselves in the prosaic form of steam locomotive and the electric telegraph.

Nowadays, everybody has travelled to some distant land, has seen, with everybody's eyes, the charmed isles and lotus shores that used to be only in books. In this lively, changing age everybody is living his own romance. And this is why the romance of story grows pale and is thrown aside. A domestic sketch of everyday life, of outward calm and simplicity, soothes the unrest of active life, and charms more than three volumes of wild incident that cannot equal the excitement that every reader is enacting in his own drama.

There were as many romances in life around me, that night, as there were persons in the theatre. I had not merely learned that the cold Aurelia was passionately in love, that the gay Lilly was broken-hearted, that the frank Annette was silly, and Angelina and Frank engaged before it was out. Beside all this, I had learned the trials and joys of many others whom I know only in this way; and I left the theatre the last, as I had come in the first.

The next morning I returned to business affairs again. It

was a particularly pressing morning. The steamer was in. I had not even time to think of my last night's experiences. Only at the corner of a street I met an acquaintance, whose smiling face amazed me. I knew that all last evening his mind had been preoccupied with the truly critical state of his affairs, and I was at a loss how to greet him. He hurried away from my embarrassment. I had more than one of these encounters; but it was not till the labors of the day were over that I understood how my knowledge of mankind had been lately increased. I went, in the evening, to a small party where I knew I should meet the Seymours. I fell in there with Aurelia first. She was as cold and as stately as ever. I entered into conversation with her, feeling that I could touch the key-note of her life. But no; she was as chilling to me as ever; nothing warmed her – nothing elicited from her the slighest spark. Sometimes she looked at me a little wonderingly, as if I were talking in some style unusual to me; as if my remarks were, in a manner, impertinent; but, in the end, I left her to her icy coldness.

As for Lilly, she appeared to the world, in general, as gay as ever. I fancied I detected a slight listlessness as she accompanied her partner into the dancing-room for the sixth polka. It was no great help with me in talking to Annette, that I knew she was a fool. I won no thanks from Frank or Angelina when I manoeuvred that they should have a little flirtation in the library. For some reason they were determined that their engagement should not be apparent, and I was reproached afterwards by Frank for my clumsiness, and received, in return, no confidences to make up for the reproach.

On the whole I passed a disagreeable evening. I had a feeling all the time that I was in the presence of smothered volcanoes, and a consciousness that I had the advantage of the rest of the world in knowing all its secret history. This became, at last, almost insupportable.

There was no opera this night. The next day it was announced that Mademoiselle—Would take her accustomed place in the performance. I went early to the theatre, and found, to my amazement, there had been some changes made in the orchestra; the prompter's box had been enlarged, and my newly discovered niche had been rendered inaccessible and almost entirely filled in! In vain did I attempt to find some other position that might correspond to it. I only attracted the attention of the early comers to the theatre. I was obliged to return to my old position of an outside observer of life, and see, quite unoccupied, that centre of all observation which I had enjoyed myself so much two nights before; over which the leader of the orchestra was unconsciously waving his baton.

I made some inquiries for Marie. One day I went down

the quiet, secluded street, where they told me she lived. I walked up and down before the house. It was very tantalising to feel that I had no excuse for approaching her. Of all the figures that had assembled around me that night, hers had remained the most distinct upon my memory. For, through the whole, she had retained an outward bearing which had corresponded with what I could see of her inward self. Even when she threw herself most earnestly into her part, she had scarcely seemed to lose herself. She had always remained a simple, self-devoted girl.

I longed to see more of her. I wanted to see her in that quiet home. While I was wandering up and down, I abused the forms of society which would make my beginning an acquaintance with her so difficult. I saw Franz, brother Franz, the flute-player, leave the house. Scarcely conscious of what I was doing, I went, as soon as he had left the street, to the door which was open to all comers; to the house which contained more than one family. I made my way up stairs and knocked at the door to which Franz's card was attached.

It was opened by Marie. She stood before me with a handkerchief tied over her head, and a broom in her hand, but she looked, to me, as beautiful as she had done behind the glare of the footlights. Her simplicity was here even more fascinating.

She held the door partly open, while I, to recover myself,

asked for Franz. She told me he was gone out, but would return soon, if I would wait for him. I was never less anxious to see any person than then to see Franz, but I could not resist entering the room, and this, in spite of the apologetic air of Marie. The room looked as neat as I had imagined it, seeing it from the mirror of Marie's mind. I should say it scarcely needed that broom which still remained expectantly in Marie's hand. A piano, spider-legged, in the number and thinness of these supports, stood at one side of the room, weighed down with classic-looking music. A bouquet, that had been given by the hand of the prima donna to Marie, stood upon the piano.

Otherwise it was a common enough looking room. Some remark being necessary, I inquired of Franz's health, and hoped he was not wearing himself out with hard work; I had seen him regularly at the opera. Marie encouraged me with regard to her brother's health, and still, the opera even did not serve to open a conversation with Marie.

Then, indeed, did I wish that I was the hero of a novel. I might have told her I was writing an opera, and have asked her to study for its heroine. I might have retired, and sent her, directly and mysteriously, a grand piano of the very grandest scale. Or, I might have asked her to sit down to that old-fashioned instrument, and have asked her to let me hear her sing, for my nieces were in need of a new teacher.

I might have engaged Franz, with promise of a high salary, to write me the music of songs, or a new sonata. But I had neither the salary nor the nieces. I had not even an excuse for standing there. It was very foolish of me, but I could not help feeling that it was exceedingly impertinent of me to be there.

Instead of informing Marie that I was intimately acquainted with her, that I had shared every emotion of her soul, on the exciting opera night, I stated that I could call again upon brother Franz. I regretted, at the same time, that I had not my card, and left the room with a courteous bow of dismissal from Marie.

I have walked that way very often. Once or twice I have seen Marie at the window, when she has not seen me. But I have not attempted to visit her again. Of what use is it for me, then, to have such a knowledge of her, when she does not have a similar one sympathetic with me? She has not sung in public of late, and I do not know the reason why she has not.

My friends are fond of asking me why I, every night, sit in a different place at the theatre; and why I have such a fancy for a seat in the midst of the trumpets of the orchestra, and directly under the leader. I am striving to make new acoustic discoveries.

But I dare not state in what theatre it is that my point of

observation can be found, not ask of the management to make an alteration in the position of the orchestra, lest some night I should be observed, and expose all the secrets of my breast to a less confidential observer.

A SHOT AT THE SUN

M. P. Shiel

SUPERNATURAL

'Brownrigg risked terrible vengeance by firing at the sun
– a story of the old slavery days.'
The Pictorial Magazine, 1903.

I tell you something which I have seen with my own eyes;
you believe it or not, as you like.

I am an old fellow now at this date of writing, and what
I tell of happened forty years ago, in the old slavery days,
down South.

Charles K. Brownrigg at that time was the owner of
two hundred and forty-five niggers, not to mention fifteen
hundred acres of cotton plantation. And I take it upon me
to state that he was the worst-shunned and the worst-feared
man in the Southern States of America.

He was a big, red man, with hard, hairless jaws and a goat-
beard, and continually went about with a gun on his shoulder.

His estate house, a rambling place, lay a little outside of Cliftonville (in South Carolina), and looked directly upon his plantations. That gun wjiich he carried had shot, at one time or another, five separate niggers – nobody had the least doubt of it in Cliftonville – yet by some strange power which was in him, or about him, Brownrigg had escaped justice.

One day – it was in 'the hot' of the year '59 – a maroon rushed into the shed where Brownrigg was overseeing the reaping, with the words:

'Massa, massa, Brams and Jess done gone run 'way!'

Brams was a negro youth of twenty, and Jess a mulatto, girl, shapely as Venus, both slaves of Brownrigg. Brams and Jess, from the first mutual glance some months before had loved; and now, by concert, had taken to the woods and wilds in some mad hope of finding free happiness.

Brownrigg's Panama hat was low on his forehead that morning, and his face even before this announcement had worn a scowl, for he was in money difficulties; he had had two bad years with the cotton, and as the news of the flight passed the lips of the maroon Brownrigg sent the long lash of a short-handled cowhide coiling about the man's legs with the crack of a Maxim gun, while the slave skipped in a dance of pain.

There was something very queer about Brownrigg – he was no ordinary slave-owner. Now, for instance, when he threw down the whip, and the slave lay writhing in the 'long-grass', it was natural to expect that he would have rushed instantly away, hurried together dogs and horses, and set out after the fugitives. But he did nothing of the sort.

What he did do was to put his hand into his waistcoat-pocket, draw out three little black stones, deposit them in his left palm, and stare at them for some three minutes. They were obiah-stones.

Brownrigg, standing with his knickered bowlegs apart, put a finger-tip to his lips, touched each of the stones with spittle, and rattled them in his left hand. Then he opened the hand, put the middle stone back into his pocket, and with two fingers of the right hand struck down smartly upon the two remaining stones. They started away from his palm in divergent directions; Brownrigg noted the directions and picked them up.

Only then did he set out. He hurried to the estate house, blowing a whistle. In ten minutes two pursuing parties had started in the directions which the stones had indicated, and in less than an hour Brams and Jess were safely lodged in the estate ward-house. It may have been only chance, or it may have been Brownrigg's obiah-stones, that caught them; of course, I do not know – I merely state facts.

Brams and Jess were to be pitied that day, if ever two poor mortals were to be pitied. I say that day, meaning that day above all other days whatsoever; for on that day Brownrigg had in him the humour of ten demons. I am going to tell you why. Perhaps you are aware that there are three special days (sometimes it is four, or even five, but usually it is three) when, during the cotton-reap, it is of the greatest importance that the sun shine strongly and steadily, without rain or even cloud. Cloud means loss, rain disaster, the reason being that the new-plucked fruit needs just at that time the swelter of the sun for what is called its 'fibring'. Now this particular day when Brams and Jess ran away and were captured was the second of the three critical days in that year, and the sun was not shining too well, and Brownrigg was angry with it.

You may imagine perhaps that the sun did not care so very much about Brownrigg's anger, but this was the very point which was in doubt all through Clifton ville that day; and it is no exaggeration to say that positively hundreds of bets were being made in the saloons, in the Exchange, at the store doors, as to whether the sun would shine, and, if not, as to whether Brownrigg would command it to shine, and, in that case, as to whether or not it would obey Brownrigg.

The fact is that during the previous year's reap, one afternoon, when the sun had gone behind a cloud, Brownrigg had been clearly seen to do an extraordinary thing. Standing in midfield he had hurriedly loaded his gun; he had then cocked the hammer ready for shooting; then he had taken his massive silver watch in his left hand, and three niggers near had heard him say, with a nod of the sun, these strange words:

'I give you five minutes!'

And one minute, two, three minutes passed, and the sun had remained hidden; and four minutes had passed, and it had remained hidden; and as the five minutes ended it had walked out into open sky with clear, blistering face.

Now Cliftonville was not a bit more superstitious than anywhere else, and in another man such conduct would have seemed to it simply silly. But in Brownrigg it somehow did not seem silly. He was felt to be a genuinely diabolical and dreadful man. It was known for a certainty that with blackened face he had attended the rites and midnight orgies of the negro obiah-men in the depths of the forest. All Cliftonville knew it. And at the top of his estate house was some sort of cupola in which at night his light was seen to shine, no one knowing in the least what Brownrigg was doing there – whether he was star-gazing, or whether he was holding intercourse with who can say what or whom.

And therefore, I say, the bets in Cliftonville were many that day, and a thrill of excitement filled the town; and when, about two in the afternoon, the sun went definitely behind a spread of cloud, looking as if it meant to stay there and casting a shade over the land, all the lanes leading to

Brownrigg's plantation were covered with groups of twos and threes, of fives and tens, slouching out innocently that way to see what there was to see.

At that hour Brownrigg was with the two runaways in a foul hole of the estate ward-house – he and they were alone. He had tied them together with many whorls of rope which entered the flesh, and he had laid them so upon the mud floor, with outstretched arms. At his feet were two pails of boiling water, whose surface still bubbled, and in his hand his gun.

'Now, you two young niggers!' was all he said.

Upon the two forms he tossed in three spurts the contents of one pail, the tied mass on the floor filling the cell with yells and flinging itself about in wriggling spasms. Then he put down the pail, took from his waistcoat-pocket one of the little obiah-stones, spat on it, dropped it into the other pail, and said these words aloud:

'I give the lives of these two young niggers for a good reap. The moment that water cools, let 'em die, Bam, let 'em die, O Bam.'

Then Brownrigg put his gun to his shoulder and took aim. He had not the least intention of killing, for slave justice, though crude, was yet an existent fact, and he had been too often suspected of murder already. But he took aim; he was a good shot, and though the den was dark he could see. He sighted the fleshy parts of the now quietly-groaning mass.

He pierced the shoulder of Brams; a minute, then ping! – he pierced the thigh of Jess; another minute, then ping! – he pierced he knew not what, for at this third shot the gun gave such a jarring kick at his shoulder that he staggered backward. The shock was very unexpected. He frowned.

'Why, what's matter with the old gun?' he muttered.

He cast a glance at the pail containing the stone, shouldered his gun, and ascended. As he mounted the light shone on a hideous face distorted with passions.

The first thing he saw now was that the sun was not shining as it should.

He at once went down the back-lane toward the plantation, around he cast his lurid eyes, and must have observed that every path and niche of foliage was thronged with people from Cliftonville. But he took no interest in them. All along the cotton overseer and nigger were at work – but in shadow – the sun was behind a cloud.

Every minute Brownrigg was losing seventy-five dollars.

All eyes were fixed upon Brownrigg. All about him was a murmur of tongues. Bets ran high. Brownrigg seemed unconscious of it all.

Suddenly, with a jerk, he moved. He put his left hand to his waistcoat-pocket.

This was a signal for a general crowding round him;

through field and path they came, everyone, however, keeping a respectable distance.

There was a rock near to Brownrigg, and on the top of this he put his watch, together with the leather strap which attached it to his waistcoat. Face upward he settled it, just under his eye; and he put his gun to his shoulder, and with a face of diabolical wickedness he pointed it at the sun.

As he did so he said these words:

'Three minutes – I give you three.'

The words were heard by an overseer who at that moment had happened to approach Brownrigg. And the overseer, holding down his little finger with his thumb, lifted on high three fingers behind Brownrigg's back to show the crowd how the matter stood.

At once hundreds of watches were snatched from hundreds of pockets, and held in hundreds of palms. A minute passed. Not a sound now but the soft rush of the breeze in the cotton leafage, every man feeling his heart beat thickly in his bosom.

The second minute is gone. The sun remains clouded, and steadily points Brownrigg's muzzle at it. Every five or six seconds he gives a downward glance at his watch. In all that crowd of onlookers there is hardly now a single face not pallid with excitement.

Suddenly there is a stirring – there is the wildest sensation!

The sun is re-adjusting itself – there is a working, a movement yonder on high – the clouds are giving way, as when a crowd opens for the passage of Royalty! He has won his way – he shines triumphantly – the world is sweltering in his blaze.

From the fields and lanes there went up a shout. Brownrigg was seen to nod, as if to say, 'Ah, so much the better for you!' There were still fifteen seconds lacking to the completion of his three minutes.

During the next five minutes there ensued an agitated scene among the crowd; bets were being settled, comments made; on the outskirts there was a tendency toward departure for Cliftonville. It seemed probable that the saloons would do a brisk trade that day, for considerable sums had changed hands.

Brownrigg had again put on his watch. He was talking to the overseer who had approached him. In the midst of his talk he was seen to snatch up his cow-skin 'cart-whip', and crack it round the bare legs of a negro who had happened to pass too near.

All at once those who had sauntered from the outskirts of the crowd to return to the town stopped, and ran back with cries to their former stations. With a strange suddenness the sun had buried itself into cloud, involving the land in shadow.

Expectation now stood more wildly on tiptoe than ever.

The betting instinct at this fresh impetus was on the point of manifesting itself with tenfold vigour; but, as a matter of fact, not a single bet was made, for Brownrigg left them no time. With a gesture of horrible rage he snatched away his watch, placed it on the stone, snatched up his gun, and pointed it upward.

The overseer, still near him, drew away, and, holding down his third and fourth fingers with his thumb, lifted on high his first two behind Brownrigg's back for the information of the crowd. Brownrigg had said:

'Two minutes – I give you two.'

And once more the hundreds of watches lay flat in the hundreds of palms. And in silence a minute passed.

It must have been about this time, as the Cliftonville folk said afterwards, that the negro Brams drew himself along the mud floor of his cell, wounded as he was, dragging with him his companion in misery. He had heard the curse pronounced against him, and seen the obiah-stone dropped into the hot water. With a push he upset the pail, and took out the stone. That is what he afterwards asserted.

But whatever truth is to be credited to the statement of the black, the fact remains that Brownrigg stood with gun pointed at the sun; and a minute passed and the sun remained hidden.

Obstinately this time. A minute and a half – and no one

dared to breathe; a sense of the awful oppressed the heart; the waiting air seemed crowded with something momentous. The breeze died away, as if holding its breath to watch that blasphemy.

Then – at last – with a shock of fear everyone knew that the two minutes were over, and the sun remained a mere blotch.

Bang! Brownrigg fired.

He vanished. He perished. Never could one have conceived such a thing. To say that the gun burst and sent him into eternity is to put it very feebly: *he disappeared.* Gun and Brownrigg and watch were wiped out. The folk at Cliftonville used to tell that not a single trace was left of him – that he was clean eaten up and swallowed by the wrath of heaven. That is an exaggeration – but not much of one; some traces were found – but *wonderfully* few. I state facts.

DELENDA EST

Robert E. Howard

OUTRÉ

*'The tall, dark stranger disturbed the Vandal's mind . . .
until he realised just who he was.' A forgotten story by the
master of fantasy.*

'It's no empire, I tell you! It's only a sham. Empire? Pah!
Pirates, that's all we are!' It was Hunegais, of course, the
ever moody and gloomy, with his braided black locks and
drooping moustaches betraying his Slavonic blood. He
sighed gustily, and the Falernian wine slopped over the rim
of the jade goblet clenched in his brawny hand, to stain his
purple, gilt-embroidered tunic. He drank noisily, after the
manner of a horse, and returned with melancholy gusto to
his original complaint.

'What have we done in Africa? Destroyed the big
landholders and the priests, set ourselves up as landlords.
Who works the land? Vandals? Not at all! The same men

who worked it under the Romans. We've merely stepped into Roman shoes. We levy taxes and rents, and are forced to defend the land from the accursed Berbers. Our weakness is in our numbers. We can't amalgamate with the people! We'd be absorbed. We can't make allies ahd subjects out of them; all we can do is maintain a sort of military prestige – we are a small body of aliens sitting in castles and, for the present, enforcing our rule over a big native population – who, it's true, hates us no worse than they hated the Romans, but—'

'Some of that hate could be done away with,' interrupted Athaulf. He was younger than Hunegais, clean-shaven, and not unhandsome; his manners were less primitive. He was a Suevi, whose youth had been spent as a hostage in the East Roman court. 'They are orthodox; if we could bring ourselves to renounce Arianism—'

No! Hunegais' heavy jaws came together with a snap that would have splintered lesser teeth than his. His dark eyes flamed with the fanaticism that was, among all the Teutons, the exclusive possession of his race. 'Never! We are the masters! It is theirs to submit – not ours. We *know* the truth of Arian; if the miserable Africans can not realise their mistake, they must be made to see it – by torch and sword and rack, if necessary!' Then his eyes dulled again, and with another gusty sigh from the depths of his belly, he groped for the wine jug.

'In a hundred years the Vandal kingdom will be a memory,' he predicted. 'All that holds it together now is the will of Genseric.' He pronounced it Geiserich.

The individual so named laughed, leaned back in his carven ebony chair, and stretched out his muscular legs before him. Those were the legs of a horseman; but their owner had exchanged the saddle for the deck of a war galley. Within a generation, he had turned a race of horsemen into a race of sea-rovers. He was the king of a race whose name had already become a term for destruction, and he was the possessor of the finest brain in the known world.

Born on the banks of the Danube and grown to manhood on that long trek westward, when the drifts of the nations crushed over the Roman palisades, he had brought to the crown forged for him in Spain all the wild wisdom the times could teach, in the feasting of swords and the surge and crush of races. His wild riders had swept the spears of the Roman rulers of Spain into oblivion. When the Visigoths and the Romans joined hands and began to look southward, it was the intrigues of Genseric which brought Attila's scarred Huns swarming westward, tusking the flaming horizons with their myriad lances. Attila was dead now, and none knew where lay his bones and his treasures, guarded by the ghosts of five hundred slaughtered slaves; his name thundered around the world; but in his day he had been but one of the pawns moved resistlessly by the hand of the Vandal king.

And when, after Ghalons, the Gothic hosts moved down through the Pyrenees, Genseric had not waited to be crushed by superior numbers. Men still cursed the name of Boniface, who called on Genseric to aid him against his rival, Aetius, and opened the Vandal's road to Africa. His reconciliation with Rome had been too late; vain as the courage with which he had sought to undo what he had done. Boniface died on a Vandal spear, and a new kingdom rose in the south. And now Aetius, too, was dead, and the great war galleys of the Vandals were moving northward, the long oars dipping and flashing silver in the starlight, the great vessels heeling and rocking to the lift of the waves.

And in the cabin of the foremost galley, Genseric listened to the conversation of his captains, and smiled gently as he combed his unruly yellow beard with his muscular fingers. There was in his veins no trace of the Scy thic blood which set his race somewhat aside from the other Teutons, from the long ago when scattered steppes-riders, drifting westward before the. conquering Sarmatians, had come among the people dwelling on the upper reaches of the Elbe. Genseric was pure German; of medium height, with a magnificent sweep of shoulders and chest, and a massive corded neck, his frame promised as much of physical vitality as his wide blue eyes reflected mental vigor.

He was the strongest man in the known world, and he was a pirate – the first of the Teutonic sea-raiders whom men later called Vikings; but his domain of conquest was not the Baltic nor the blue North Sea, but the sunlit shores of the Mediterranean.

'And the will of Genseric,' he laughed, in reply to Hunegais' last remark, 'is that we drink and feast and let tomorrow take care of itself.'

'So you say!' snorted Hunegais, with the freedom that still existed among the barbarians. 'When did you ever let a tomorrow take care of itself? You plot and plot, not for tomorrow alone, but for a thousand tomorrows to come! You need not masquerade with us! We are not Romans to be fooled into thinking *you* are a fool – as Boniface was!'

'Aetius was no fool,' muttered Thrasamund.

'But he's dead, and we are sailing on Rome,' answered Hunegais, with the first sign of satisfaction he had yet evinced. 'Alaric didn't get all the loot, thank God! And I'm glad Attila lost his nerve at the last minute – the more plunder for us.'

'Attila remembered Chalons,' drawled Athaulf. 'There is something about Rome that lives – by the saints, it is strange. Even when the empire seems most ruined – torn, befouled, and tattered – some part of it springs into life again. Stilicho, Theodosius, Aetius – who can tell? Tonight in Rome there may be a man sleeping who will overthrow us all.'

Hunegais snorted and hammered on the wine-stained board.

'Rome is as dead as the white mare I rode at the taking of Carthage! We have but to stretch out our hands and grasp the plunder of her!'

'There was a great general once who thought as much,' said Thrasamund drowsily. 'A Carthaginian, too, by God! I have forgotten his name. But he beat the Romans at every turn. Cut, slash, that was his way!'

'Well,' remarked Hunegais, 'he must have lost at last, or he would have destroyed Rome.'

'That's so!' ejaculated Thrasamund.

'We are not Carthaginians,' laughed Genseric. 'And who said aught of plundering Rome? Are we not merely sailing to the imperial city in answer to the appeal of the Empress who is beset by jealous foes? And now, get out of here, all of you. I want to sleep.'

The cabin door slammed on the morose predictions of Hunegais, the witty retorts of Athaulf, the mumble of the others. Genseric rose and moved over to the table, to pour himself a last glass of wine. He walked with a limp; a Frankish spear had girded him in the leg long years ago.

He lifted the jeweled goblet to his lips – wheeled with a startled oath. He had not heard the cabin door open, but a man was standing across the table from him.

'By Odin!' Genseric's Arianism was scarcely skin-deep. 'What do you in my cabin?'

The voice was calm, almost placid, after the first startled oath. The king was too shrewd to often evince his real emotions. His hand stealthily closed on the hilt of his sword. A sudden and unexpected stroke—

But the man made no hostile movement. He was a stranger to Genseric, and the Vandal knew he was neither Teuton nor Roman. He was tall, dark, with a stately head, his flowing locks confined by a dark crimson band. A curling, patriarchal beard swept his breast. A dim, misplaced familiarity twitched at the Vandal's mind as he looked.

'I have not come to harm you!' The voice was deep, strong, and resonant. Genseric could tell little of his attire, since he was masked in a wide dark cloak. The Vandal wondered if he grasped a weapon under that cloak.

'Who are you, and how did you get into my cabin?' he demanded.

'Who I am, it matters not,' returned the other. 'I have been on this ship since you sailed from Carthage. You sailed at night; I came aboard then.'

'I never saw you in Carthage,' muttered Genseric. 'And you are a man who would stand out in a crowd.'

'I dwell in Carthage,' the stranger replied. 'I have dwelt there for many years. I was born there, and my forefathers before me. Carthage is my life!' The last sentence was uttered in a voice so passionate and fierce that Genseric involuntarily stepped back, his eyes narrowing.

'The folk of the city have some cause of complaint against us,' said he. 'But the looting and destruction was not by my orders. Even then it was my interition to make Carthage my capital. If you suffered loss by the sack, why—'

'Not from your wolves,' grimly answered the other. 'Sack of the city? I have seen such a sack as not even you, barbarian, have dreamed of! They call you barbaric. I have seen what civilised Romans can do.'

'Romans have not plundered Carthage in my memory,' muttered Genseric, frowning in some perplexity.

'Poetic justice!' cried the stranger, his hand emerging from his cloak to strike down on the table. Genseric noted that the hand was muscular yet white, the hand of an aristocrat. 'Roman greed and treachery destroyed Carthage, trade rebuilt her in another guise. Now you, barbarian, sail from her harbors to humble her conqueror! Is it any wonder that old dreams silver the cords of your ships and creep amidst the holds, and that forgotten ghosts burst their immemorial tombs to glide upon your decks?'

'Who said anything of humbling Rome?' uneasily demanded Genseric. 'I merely sail to arbitrate a dispute as to succession—'.

'Pah!' Again the hand slammed down on the table. 'If you knew what I know, you would sweep that accursed city clean of life before you turn your prows southward again. Even now, those you sail to aid plot your ruin – and a traitor is on board your ship!'

'What do you mean?' Still there was neither excitement nor passion in the Vandal's voice.

'Suppose I gave you proof that your most trusted companion and vassal plots your ruin with those to whose aid you lift your sails?'

'Give me that proof; then ask what you will,' answered Genseric with a touch of grimness.

'Take this in token of faith!' The stranger rang a coin on the table, and caught up a silken girdle which Genseric himself had carelessly thrown down.

'Follow me to the cabin of your counsellor and scribe, the handsomest man among the barbarians—'

'Athaulf?' In spite of himself, Genseric started. 'I trust him beyond all others.'

'Then you are not as wise as I deemed you,' grimly answered the other. 'The traitor within is to be feared more than the foe without. It was not the legions of Rome which conquered *me* – it was the traitors within my gates. Not alone in swords and ships does Rome deal, but with the souls of men. I have come from a far land to save your empire and your life. In return I ask but one thing: drench Rome in blood!'

For an instant the stranger stood transfigured, mighty arm lifted, fist clenched, dark eyes flashing fire. An aura of terrific power emanated from him, awing even the wild Vandal. Then sweeping his purple cloak about him with a kingly gesture, the man stalked to the door and through it, despite Genseric's exclamation and effort to detain him.

Swearing in bewilderment, the king limped to the door, opened it, and glared out on the deck. A lamp burned on the poop. A reek of unwashed bodies came up from the hold where the weary rowers toiled at their oars. The rhythmic clack vied with a dwindling chorus from the ships which followed in a long ghostly line. The moon struck silver from the waves, shone white on the deck. A single warrior stood on guard outside Genseric's door, the moonlight sparkling on his crested golden helmet and Roman corselet. He lifted his javelin in salute.

'Where did he go?' demanded the king.

'Who, my lord?' inquired the warrior stupidly.

'The tall man, dolt,' exclaimed Genseric impatiently. 'The man in the purple cloak who just left my cabin.'

'None has left your cabin since the lord Hugenais and the others went forth, my lord,' replied the Vandal in bewilderment.

'Liar!' Genseric's sword was a ripple of silver in his hand as it slid from its sheath. The warrior paled and shrank back.

'As God is my witness, king,' he swore, 'no such man have I seen this night.'

Genseric glared at him; the Vandal king was a judge of men and he knew this one was not lying. He felt a peculiar twitching of his scalp, and turning without a word, limped hurriedly to Athaulf's cabin. There he hesitated, then threw open the door.

Athaulf lay sprawled across a table in an attitude which needed no second glance to classify. His face was purple, his glassy eyes distended, and his tongue lolled out blackly. About his neck, knotted in such a knot as seamen make, was Genseric's silken girdle. Near one hand lay a quill, near the other, ink and a piece of parchment. Catching it up, Genseric read laboriously.

To her majesty, the empress of Rome:

I, thy faithful servant, have done thy bidding, and am prepared to persuade the barbarian I serve to delay his onset on the imperial city until the aid you expect from Byzantium has arrived. Then I will guide him into the bay I mentioned, where he can be caught as in a vise and destroyed with his whole fleet, and—

The writing ceased with an erratic scrawl. Genseric glared down at him, and again the short hairs lifted on his scalp. There was no sign of the tall stranger, and the Vandal knew he would never be seen again.

'Rome shall pay for this,' he muttered. The mask he wore in public had fallen away; the Vandal's face was that of a hungry wolf. In his glare, in the knotting of his mighty hand, it took no sage to read the doom of Rome. He suddenly remembered that he still clutched in his hand the coin the stranger had dropped on his table. He glanced at it, and his breath hissed between his teeth, as he recognised the characters of an old, forgotten language, the features of a man which he had often seen carved in ancient marble in old Carthage, preserved from Roman hate.

'Hannibal!' muttered Genseric.

CLAUDE FARRÈRE

Frédéric-Charles Bargone – who wrote under the pseudonym Claude Farrère – was born in Lyon, France in 1876. Initially, he followed his father into the naval academy, eventually rising to the rank of captain in 1918. However, he resigned the next year to concentrate full-time on writing. Bargone was a prolific author, penning more than sixty novels and numerous short stories, many set in exotic locations throughout Asia and the Middle East. *Les Civilisés* (*The Civilized*) won the prestigious Prix Goncourt for 1905. However, Bargone has somewhat fallen our of favour in recent times, and almost none of his works remain in print.

FRED M. WHITE

Frederick Merrick White was born in 1859. He wrote a large amount of short stories during his lifetime, and although most of these have been largely forgotten, the six that make up his 'Doom of London' series remain widely-anthologised.First published in *Pearson's Magazine*, these include 'The Four Days' Night' (1903), in which London is plagued by killer smog; 'The Dust of Death' (1903), in which deadly diphtheria infects the city; and The Four White Days' (1903), in which a sudden and harsh winter paralyses the city under snow and ice.

EDGAR ALLAN POE

Edgar Allan Poe was born in Boston, Massachusetts in 1809. He was left an orphan at a very young age, following the abscondence of his father and subsequent death of his mother, but was taken in by a couple from Richmond, Virginia. After a brief spell living in England and Scotland, Poe enrolled at the newly-established University of Virginia. However, after just one semester, having become estranged from his foster father due to gambling debts, and finding himself unable to fund his studies, he dropped out. In 1827, aged 18, Poe travelled back to Boston, the city of his birth.

By now in severe financial trouble, Poe lied about his age in order to enlist in the army. After spending two years posted to South Carolina, and having failed as an officer's cadet at West Point, Poe left the military by getting deliberately court-martialled. He left for New York in 1831, where he released his third collection of poems, the first two having received almost zero attention. Not long after its publication, in March of 1831, Poe returned to Baltimore.

From 1831 onwards, Poe began in earnest to try and make a living as a writer, and turned from poetry to prose. Despite often finding himself penniless, and frequently having to move city to stay in employment as a critic, during the thirties and forties Poe published a good amount of fiction.

Most of his best known short-stories, such as 'The Tell Tale Heart,' 'Ligeia', 'William Wilson' and 'The Fall of the House of Usher', were published between 1835 and 1845. In January 1845, Poe published his poem 'The Raven', which – despite fact that he only received $9 for it – was a great success, turning him overnight into something of a household name.

Poe died in 1849, aged just 40. The circumstances were somewhat odd; he was found wandering the streets of Baltimore at five in the morning, delirious and wearing someone else's clothes, and he repeatedly cried out "Reynolds!" during the hours before his death. The cause of death remains a mystery, with everything from epilepsy to rabies cited. However, whatever the reason behind his unusual passing, Poe's legacy is a formidable one: He is seen today as one of the greatest practitioners of Gothic and detective fiction that ever lived, and popular culture is replete with references to him.

FITZ JAMES O'BRIEN

Fitz James O'Brien was born in County Cork, Ireland in 1828. He attended the University of Dublin, where he showed an enthusiasm for writing verse, and upon graduating moved to London. In 1852, he emigrated to the USA to dedicate his life to writing, and had his early work published in *Lantern* magazine. From February of 1853, he began to work with *Harper's Magazine*, and went to on write for a number of other publications, including *Vanity Fair* and the *Atlantic* Although he penned a vast amount of articles, and even plays, O'Brien is chiefly remembered nowadays for a number of much-anthologized stories he wrote: 'The Diamond Lens', his most famous short story, can be regarded as a forerunner of the sciencefiction genre; 'What Was It?' is alleged to have served as a model for H.G. Wells' 'The Invisible Man'; and The Wondersmith' is an early example of the 'robot rebellion' plotline later popularised by writers such as Arthur C. Clarke and Phillip K. Dick. O'Brien died in 1862, from wounds sustained while fighting in the American Civil War.

M. P. SHIEL

M. P. Shiel was born in Plymouth, the West Indies in 1865. He studied classics at King's College, London, and upon graduating made the acquaintance of Oscar Wilde and Arthur Machen. After working as a mathematics teacher for two years, Shiel had his first writing success with the 1895 three-part story *Prince Zaleski*. He followed this a year later with his collection *Stones in the Fire* (1896), which includes his best-known fantasy story 'Xelucha'.

By this point a popular and well-read author, Shiel released his popular *The Yellow Danger*, in 1899. Playing on the popular fear of Eastern power and immigration, the novel, along with similar later works such as *The Dragon* (1913), is often credited with the creation of the xenophobic phrase 'the yellow peril'. Shiel also wrote historical romances, such as *The Man Stealers* (1900), before turning to science-fiction with his best-known novel, *The Purple Cloud* (1901). He even found time to pen a series of detective stories as 'Gordon Holmes', which included the novels *By Force of Circumstance* (1910), and *The House of Silence* (1911). Shiel died in 1947, aged 81. His legacy is a mixed one; he is seen as both an exuberant genre-innovator and a somewhat sad, xenophobic figure. His *Times* obituary described him as "a master of fantasy, less widely known than he deserves."

ROBERT E. HOWARD

Robert Ervin Howard was born in Peaster, Texas in 1906. During his youth, his family moved between a variety of Texan boomtowns, and Howard – a bookish and somewhat introverted child – was steeped in the violent myths and legends of the Old South. Although he loved reading and learning, Howard developed a distinctly Texan, hardboiled outlook on the world. He became a passionate fan of boxing, taking it up at an amateur level, and from the age of nine began to write adventure tales of semi-historical bloodshed. In 1919, when Howard was thirteen, his family moved to the Central Texas hamlet of Cross Plains, where he would stay for the rest of his life.

At fifteen Howard began to read the pulp magazines of the day, and to write more seriously. The December 1922 issue of his high school newspaper featured two of his stories, 'Golden Hope Christmas' and 'West is West'. In 1924 he sold his first piece – a short caveman tale titled 'Spear and Fang' – for $16 to the not-yet-famous *Weird Tales* magazine. He published with the magazine regularly over the next few years. 1929 was a breakout year for Howard, in that the 23-year-old writer began to sell to other magazines, such as *Ghost Stories* and *Argosy*, both of whom had previously sent him hundreds of rejection slips. In 1930, he began a correspondence with weird fiction master H. P. Lovecraft which ran up to his death six years later, and is regarded as one of the great correspondence cycles in all of fantasy literature.

It was partly due to Lovecraft's encouragement that Howard created his most famous character, Conan the Cimmerian. Conan – a barbarian-turned-King during the Hyborian Age, a mythical period of some 12,000 years ago – featured in seventeen *Weird Tales* stories between 1933 and 1936, and is now regarded as having spawned the 'sword and sorcery' genre, making Howard's influence on fantasy literature comparable to that of J. R. R. Tolkien's. The Conan stories have since been adapted many times, most famously in the series of films starring Arnold Schwarzenegger.

Howard was enjoying an all-time high in sales by the beginning of 1936, but he was also deeply upset by the ill health of his mother, who had fallen into a coma. On the morning of June 11, 1936, he asked an attending nurse whether she would ever recover, and the nurse replied negatively. Howard walked to his car, parked outside the family home in Cross Plains, and shot himself. He died eight hours later, aged just thirty.